The Perfect Hand

Available from Amazon.com
<u>and Kindle Online Store</u>

Devouring Time

A Discerning Heart

That Truthful Place

Locker Rooms

Shall We Chat?
Revealing the Secrets of Chatting Online

For Yoko
who offered to bankroll my trip to Vegas
so I could play poker

ISBN-13:978-1517482909
ISBN-10: 1517482909

The Perfect Hand

Patty Lesser

THURSDAY

"All-in!"

The other four men at the poker table laughed so hard that their stiff-backed, cherry-wood chairs rocked backwards. Only Gary would go all-in on a five, ten, deuce flop. Everyone quickly folded their cards. Gary frowned.

As the youngest of the group at forty-three years of age, Gary Martin had immaculately combed dirty blond hair that hung softly around his tanned face and sharp hazel eyes. As usual, he was dressed in blue jeans, black t-shirt, and a black sports jacket. His wife, Anne, swore he owned over fifty pairs of jeans. Fortunately, his job as host of the radio program *Science Today* meant he could wear jeans every day.

Gary's background in science and his steady intelligence blended well together. His show was presented every day from two p.m. to five p.m. Most people listened while at work. Gary's program was educational and interesting and nothing he explained was too difficult for the average listener. Through Gary, science became something anyone could understand.

On the show, he interviewed people from all walks of life and questioned them about the environment and scientific events. It was one of the most listened to radio shows in the Boston area. Brent Laas, candidate for governor, was the focus for one program and he talked about science education in schools. As well, Frank Terkel was featured for his discussion of urban planning. Vale Noch, the foremost authority on the climate, came in to speak about climate change and predictions for the future.

Even though Gary loved interviewing people, poker was a big part of his life. He thought himself a good poker player, but he wasn't blessed with a poker face.

The five guys had been playing poker with each other for twenty-five years. While in college, they realized their science study group had other interests: namely, smoking cigars, drinking, and playing poker. They started out playing five-card stud but progressed to Texas Hold'em in light of the world's fascination with that game.

These five men shared their lives with each other. They came together when Jack almost died in a motorcycle accident and stayed by his side until his health improved. When Gary started out with his radio show, the men made sure their friends listened, which snowballed into a good-sized audience. When he opened his pharmacy, Peter's first customers were his poker buddies. They encouraged their friends to use the same pharmacy.

Each shared his marriage with his poker buddies as the men would be the groomsmen for each other. They kept Mark on his feet when his marriage dissolved. And, as each child was born, the poker buddies and their wives made sure the new parents had everything they needed. Birthdays and anniversaries were celebrated together, usually with a fun event, like paint ball, river rafting, or camping.

Every so often, without their families, the guys booked a trip to Las Vegas specifically to play poker. And, for the sole purpose of playing in poker tournaments, they spent time in the Bahamas, Louisiana, and Mississippi. On five different cruises around the Caribbean and Mexico, they played poker every night. During the day, they went their separate ways but came together at dinner.

It was Mark's turn to deal and he impeccably shuffled the fifty-two cards like a professional. Since the age of six, he had been playing card games. His grandmother had taught him to play bridge and gin rummy. Friends in high school taught him euchre, hearts, and poker. With ease, he mastered every game. He loved cards because of the science of the game. The luck factor and statistics fascinated him.

The eldest at forty-six, Mark Wadley was the only one not married. Though now a confirmed bachelor, he had a short marriage many years ago. A striking man with a six-foot frame, Mark's green eyes sparkled under well-styled light brown hair.

The poker games were always played at Mark's house. After the divorce, he bought this good-sized bungalow just on the outskirts of Boston. His black, paved driveway easily fit their three cars. (Ted and Jack had driven together.) Mark's vehicle rested in the single car garage where it could remain untouched. He loved his sleek Mercedes Sport. It had a 32V DOHC Bi-Turbo

V8 engine and could go from one to one hundred in 4.2 seconds. Top speed was 250 km/hour.

Mark worked at home as a biochemist and did some theoretical problems. Once a week, he drove to a downtown office building housing a think tank researching new organic compounds. A group of ten men and women met to discuss their results and findings. They supported each other in their endeavors.

Mark passed out the cards, then glanced at Peter whose turn it was to bet. Though they played with chips, each piece represented a monetary figure, the lowest being twenty-five cents while the dearest chip was worth two dollars.

Peter looked at his cards and called.

Gary, who always sat to Peter's right, also called. Since he wasn't an aggressive player, Gary rarely started the betting. Mark looked at his cards and decided his king and jack were good enough to start the bidding. He threw in a few of his chips to the center of the table. All the guys followed suit.

Mark dealt the flop: jack of clubs, ten of hearts, and seven of clubs. Peter and Gary checked again, but Mark pushed some chips into the pot.

"Got a jack?" Jack said as he scrutinized Mark's face. "Okay. I'll play along," and he pushed in an equal amount of chips into the pot at the center of the table.

The unofficial leader of the group was Jack Resden. He spent his days commanding children at the local highschool as a Physical Education teacher. Fitness was foremost in his mind and he felt people must start young to improve their health. He ran several miles every day and was in excellent shape.

It was difficult to argue with Jack. He was always available to talk someone into his point of view. Men were drawn to him and women flocked to him admiring not only his intelligence, but his excellent, well-conditioned six-foot-two-inch physique. His dark brown hair was cut short but not short enough to be considered military. His bright blue eyes constantly darted about ready to take the lead at any instance.

Jack was forever faithful to his wife, Ruth, and a wonderful father to his four children. He attended all their school plays and sporting events. Every evening, he helped them with their homework and prepared them for their exams. He encouraged them to experience everything in life and he made sure they had every opportunity to achieve their goals.

Though the poker players had a unique relationship, they all realized Ted and Jack had a special bond. Both men worked together at the same local high school and spent hours comparing notes on their kids. When a child had a problem, they each helped him or her. They arranged scholarships for some kids and worked with other kids having difficulties with their studies.

Ted Dunder, the Physics teacher, was married to Susan and they had three children. Jack and Ted's homes were close together and their kids often played together.

Their wives met while in nursing school. Ruth bumped into Jack at a school football game. On their first date, she invited her friend Susan and Jack brought Ted along. The couples continued their double dates and both married on June 28th, 1990. Ruth worked at the oncology care unit at the Beth Israel Deconess Medical Center while Susan worked in Pediatrics at Massachusetts General.

The others quickly folded. They knew Mark probably had a jack and they were used to Jack chasing flushes. From the way Jack tossed in his chips, the guys were betting on the flush.

Mark dealt the turn card: an ace of diamonds. He decided to bluff the ace and put in a good hunk of cash into the pot. Jack called Mark's bet without even blinking. Mark lay down the river: a deuce of clubs.

The others watched as Mark put in more chips. Jack immediately called. They turned over their cards. Mark was hoping that his jacks were still good and figured Jack was playing for a straight but Jack turned over three and ace of clubs revealing the nut flush.

"You're crazy," shouted Mark. "I hate it when you guys play that shit and win!"

That broke the table up into grunts of laughter. Ted, trying to control himself, slowly said, "I've got two words for you: Bahamas cruise."

That sent them over the top. Mark had to put his glass down fearing that he would spill its contents. Jack had won a poker tournament by playing the worst hands on the Bahama cruise seven years ago. The tournament began with 146 people. The buy-in was one hundred dollars with one rebuy until the first break.

The first to lose out of the tournament was Gary when he went head-to-head with pocket kings to a guy who held pocket aces. It was a hard way to lose. Ted got caught chasing a straight, and he was the next of their group to lose out of the tournament.

As usual Peter played cautiously and managed to stay in a long time. He lost out on a bad hand. He had no choice but to go all-in because he was the small stack and in the big blind.

Still left in the tourney were Jack and Mark who happened to be playing at the same table. The three losers turned spectators crowded around Mark and Jack's table to watch them play.

Jack won most of the hands and the guys agreed he was having a run of luck. Soon a final table was declared. One of the other players at the table took Mark out while Mark held ace-queen and the other guy had ace-king. Ace-queen was the tournament's bad luck hand. No one seemed to win with it. Mark joined the other guys to cheer Jack on.

When just three poker players remained, Jack found himself in second place. The man with the most chips was an older businessman who took the game extremely seriously. He played aggressively by constantly raising other player's bets, annoying everyone. He was out to win and grunted with anger whenever he lost a hand.

The short stack was a young man in his twenties. He was a happy-go-lucky fellow more interested in chatting with other players than playing. Jack laughed at his comments and answered now and then but didn't want to talk too much in case he gave something away to the businessman.

The kid tried to bluff the businessman and went all-in. The businessman called and won which left Jack alone at the table with him. They played a few hands betting small amounts to test each other. Both looked for tells from the other player but each had a good poker face.

But the players had different postures. Jack slumped over his cards while older man sat straight up in his seat. Their eyes didn't meet and neither did they speak.

The businessman played the big stack role and raised Jack's every bet. Jack wouldn't play his aggressive style so he didn't call those hands allowing him to steal the blinds.

When the dealer dealt the cards for the next hand, Jack found he had received a four and five of diamonds. As usual, the businessman raised doubling the pot. Jack thought, *What the hell* and raised him one-third of his stack. The businessman thought for a moment, then pushed in an equivalent amount of chips into the center of the table.

The flop, a seven of diamonds, a six of diamonds and a king of clubs, was dealt. The businessman bet half his stack. Jack wasn't about to give up a chance at a straight flush and pushed in the same amount. The turn card was a jack of hearts. He went all-in. Jack looked at his friends, winked, and called his bet.

When the dealer turned over the businessman's cards, everyone saw that he had pocket kings, giving him three-of-a-kind. A huge sigh exploded from the crowd when Jack's four and five of diamonds were revealed. Everyone held their breath as the dealer dealt the river card. The dealer turned it over slowly. It was an ace of diamonds. Jack had made his flush and won first place along with five thousand dollars.

The businessman was furious. He called Jack every bad name imaginable. Everyone laughed and the guys went over to Jack and showered him with congratulations. The businessman left the poker table in a huge huff, causing the spectators to snicker.

Back at the poker table in Mark's house, it was Jack's turn to deal. The guys continued to laugh about that Bahamas cruise until Gary pushed in half his stack for the first bet. Then the game turned serious. Mark, Jack, and Ted folded but Peter counted out the same number of chips and threw them into the center of the table. Gary ended up winning the hand when Peter chickened out after the turn.

"Anyone see last night's hockey game?" Jack asked.

The Boston Bruins had played the New York Rangers the previous evening. The five friends attended a few Bruin games in the winter, a number of Red Sox games in the summer, and Celtic games in the fall, usually taking along their kids.

"No," said Gary. "I missed it. Who won?"

"Bruins," replied the guys in unison. They laughed. Gary usually fell asleep before the end of the game.

9

Halfway through the evening, Peter left the poker table and walked into Mark's well-stocked kitchen. He took out a white ceramic dish from the hot oven and carried it over to the dining room table. The other guys took note and rose from the poker table, stretched, and then wandered into Mark's simple dining room, where a wood table, four wooden chairs and a wall cabinet stood.

Every Thursday night, the men took turns making dinner. While eating, they commented on the quality and taste of the meal. They liked to think themselves gourmets. Peter had made a casserole with shrimp, rice, raisins, mushrooms, and sherry with Swiss cheese on top.

As soon as everyone sat down at the table, Peter spooned out an ample portion to each one of his friends. They sniffed it, tasted it, and rolled their eyes. Peter prepared himself for their reviews.

"Shrimp cooked well," said Mark. "Melted in my mouth."

"Very tasty," said Ted. "Though a little sweet. Next time, leave out the raisins."

"I liked it sweet," said Gary. "Can really taste the sherry."

"Nice job, Peter. Another success," said Jack.

Peter Node was the odd man of the group. Taking a greater interest in his studies, he often brought his books to their college poker games hoping to convince the guys to study. However, more often than not, the guys got drunk and played poker into the wee hours of the early morning.

Peter was the first of the men to marry. He and his wife, Laura, met in pharmacology school and bought their own pharmacy. Not the most talkative type, he held his tongue more so now because he feared divulging patient privacies.

But, if anyone needed medical advice, Peter was the man to see. A fountain of knowledge, he studied medical journals and was an advocate for chemists prescribing medications and giving injections. He felt pharmacists should have greater responsibilities when it came to the treatment of their customers. At six-foot-three-inches, he had soft brown hair and quiet brown eyes always involved in solving some puzzle.

When Peter returned to the table after putting the leftover food away, Jack said, "I think we should go to Vegas in the fall."

"You always want to go there," said Ted. "How about another cruise?"

"Cruise to where? I'm for Vegas," said Gary rising to his feet.

"We could go to Mexico and stopover in Florida to do some fishing," answered Ted, an avid fisherman.

"I'll vote for fishing." Gary smiled.

"We'll be fishing this summer while at Jack's cottage," said Mark. "I'd like to go back to the Bellagio."

"You just want to see if that waitress is still there," said Jack.

Two years ago when they had last visited Las Vegas, Mark had met a beautiful waitress at their hotel. It was the first time Mark hadn't played as much poker as the others. He had preferred the company of Gina, a small-town girl from South Carolina, who had moved to Vegas six months before.

Mark smiled wider. He wondered if Gina still worked at the Bellagio but he also enjoyed the numerous high-stake tournaments offered at that hotel.

"Yes it's true. I'd like to see her again but it's just a great place to go and play poker," said Mark as the men returned to the table.

Jack continued to try and convince the guys to agree to Vegas over the next two hours while they played. At precisely eleven, they ceased their poker game.

Jack and Ted gathered the glasses and plates together and put them in the dishwasher. Gary collected the cards and put them in their package. Mark took care of the ashtrays, the contents of which were thrown in the garbage. Each man's tray of poker chips was placed in the wooden cabinet by Peter.

By the time the men were ready to leave, Mark's home was organized and left clean by all their efforts. They stood at the door laughing about certain hands or a comment.

Eventually, Mark was alone. He locked the front door, marched into the kitchen to turn on the dishwasher, and finished tidying up. When everything was in its proper place, he moved over to the study. He turned on his laptop to finish working on some necessary equations.

It was another good night for the men. Each one returned home happy and content after an evening of cards. Poker was their drug, their addiction. They loved the strategy and the excitement of getting lucky.

However, something was happening beyond their control. It would challenge their relationship and change their lives forever.

TUESDAY

The endless silence was suddenly interrupted by the loud tinkling of the doorbell from the front door. It angrily reverberated throughout Mark's bungalow.

Mark's aching body tensed upon hearing the disturbing noise. He had been concentrating on his work trying to synthesize an organic compound.

He glanced at the clock on his laptop: ten-fifty a.m. Three hours had lapsed since he had sat down in his study. He was due for a break. Mark slowly stretched then rose from his chair to answer the front door.

At the threshold was a UPS delivery man. He handed Mark a dull-colored package about the size of a magazine and as thick as a few fingers. Mark signed for it, carried it into his study, and placed it on his desk.

The package was wrapped in a non-descriptive, brown paper. There were no markings on the mysterious package except for the letters F, S, and C at the top left corner.

Ripping open the parcel, a thin green piece of paper, a USB stick, a number of letter-sized envelopes, and a shiny pamphlet fell out.

Flipping through the envelopes, each had the correct postage and a stamped address of a post office box in Washington, D.C. Otherwise, the white envelopes

14

were unremarkable. He put them down and glanced at the green sheet of paper.

It read:

> You have been selected to assist the FSC. Discuss this directive with no one. Send your reports weekly pertaining the movements and behaviors of your assigned individual in the enclosed self-addressed stamped envelopes. Non-compliance could prove disastrous. The USB stick reveals your mission. Keep it safe at all times. Loss of said stick could be catastrophic. We will be watching.

There was nothing else. No signature. Just a brief letterhead with FSC at the top of the plain, green sheet of paper.

When he inserted the USB stick into his computer, the name, age, address, occupation, and marital status of a woman who worked in Mark's office building were revealed. He had bumped into Marie Towsend in the building's cafeteria a few times.

He considered her to be an attractive woman with brown hair, brown eyes, and an athletic body. The stick showed her as thirty-one years old and married to Tom Towsend, a lawyer. One time, when they had stood in line together at the cafeteria, she had introduced herself as the Public Relations Supervisor in an insurance firm on the fifth floor. The stick also revealed her routine: where she shopped, her route driving to and from work, and other personal details.

Mark laughed thinking, *who were they kidding? And who in the hell was the FSC?* He googled "FSC." A plain website appeared. The background color was the same shade of green as the piece of paper with the directive on it. The site's simple bold, black letters revealed the FSC's full name as the Free Society Council.

Mark read the Free Society Council's mission statement:

> *We have the power to change Americans' lives beyond their wildest dreams by taking control of the United States and bringing true religion back.*
> *Follow us and you will be freed from the evil.*

Not believing what he read, Mark laughed again. He couldn't take this seriously. It was all too absurd. He needed to discuss this with the guys.

Sitting down in his recliner, Mark read the pamphlet last. Underneath pictures of listening devices, maps, and cameras were advertisements of places where these items could be purchased. There was a long-winded explanation on how to spy on someone and where to place small cameras and listening devices. The pamphlet also listed the best method to follow someone. Mark wondered if anyone else had received the same thing.

His body felt stiff and tense. He jumped up and checked behind his books, around the lamps, behind the paintings, and around heating grates. He located some of the small black devices advertised in the FSC's pamphlet. His hidden vault had been left undisturbed.

He left the devices where they lay because he didn't want his spy to realize he was on to him yet.

Worried about what he would find, he walked to the main front windows. With the curtain hiding him from view, he gazed about to see if anyone was around. While there was no one there, the light glittered on an object in the distance. He returned to his study and grabbed his binoculars.

He then noticed something metallic further down the road that he assumed was a car. He considered the time of day and made a mental note to check every few hours to see if that mysterious vehicle was still there. Mark was mad. How dare someone spy on him? He held great value in privacy and this invasion was not acceptable.

Because of his anger, Mark had difficulty returning to work. He sat at his desk and stared at his computer screen. He kept checking the clock and jumped up a few times to look out the window to see if the car was still there. It was. When he looked again at seven p.m., the car was gone. He then breathed a little easier.

Over the next couple of days, Mark continued his regular routine because he didn't want to provoke any suspicion. He wasn't about to allow this mysterious spy to change his life even as he kept an eye out for him. Mark placed a camcorder of his own in a discreet position when he left the house.

Upon returning home, there was a brief recording of a short, dark-skinned man entering his home and checking the listening devices Mark had discovered. Mark made plenty of notes about the intruder and kept the papers in his secure vault. He didn't want the man to realize that Mark knew about him.

Even though he handled the intruder rationally, he still felt unsettled. He didn't enjoy the thought that someone was constantly watching him.

On Thursday night, before his friends arrived, Mark removed every listening device from his home so that he could talk openly with his poker buddies about these bizarre events. Mark determined there was only one spy with a definite routine. Every afternoon for three hours, the man sat in his car just down the road. He was gone by six p.m. so Mark was assured that his friends wouldn't be overheard by the spy. He had to know if the other guys had been recruited by the FSC, causing him fear and some panicked thoughts.

THURSDAY

Another game night but things weren't the same. The atmosphere smelled of fatigue. Silence prevailed. As usual, Jack dealt the cards, but mechanically. Each man seemed distracted.

Finally Ted broke the silence, "Peter, you're looking awfully tired."

Peter looked up from his cards and with a deep sigh said, "Yeah, I've been working a lot. Time's catching up with me."

He did look tired. He had big, dark bags under his normally bright brown eyes. His light brown hair, usually so meticulously in place, was askew.

"What happened?" asked Gary with a nervous laugh. "Did everyone suddenly get sick?"

Peter gazed at Gary with sad eyes. What he said was true. More and more people were coming into his pharmacy to have prescriptions filled for anxiety and hyper-tension. He had never been so busy. He had to hire two new pharmacy technicians just to keep up with demand.

He also noted slight differences with his customers. No longer did they push for attention or talk while in line. They waited in silence, eyes down. When it was their turn, they spoke in quiet, tentative voices.

He wondered if their behaviour was due to the FSC. He had received a package from them which had scared him. Everyone else must have also received this package. It was his only guess.

The men stared at each other, almost daring the other to speak.

"I'll say it," Mark said. "I've been chosen by the FSC to spy on someone and I'm sure someone is spying on me. We can talk freely. I destroyed every listening device placed in my house."

The men looked at each other and then at Mark in wonder.

He explained how he discovered the intruder and the notes he kept regarding that man's movements. He also divulged the information about the woman he was required to spy on.

"I've been recruited too," said Gary. "I must spy on a man at the station. And I'm sure someone is spying on me."

"I've received a package too. I'm sure everyone else has received one as well so I'm sure they are also working for the FSC," said Peter.

These facts scared Ted because he hadn't received anything. "There were bugs in your house?" he asked. "Would there be any in mine?"

"I wouldn't be surprised," said Mark, shrugging his shoulders. "Someone has been in here twice but he's not very good at hiding them."

"You mean we've all got people watching us?" asked Jack, as he drank the rest of his whiskey.

"Oh, I'm sure of it," Mark said as he shuffled his chips absentmindedly. This made a clicking noise, the only sound in the room.

Gary spoke up, "About three weeks ago, I received this package in the mail. Nondescript. No return address. Inside were specifics about this guy at the radio station."

"What did you have to do?" asked Ted. He lit a cigar as he waited for Gary's response.

"I must report to the FSC once a week. At first, I thought it was just a prank. But the next day, I received a text saying where I could find my victim. I was told to report on everything he did."

"Is this happening to just us or everyone?" asked Ted, sitting up in his chair.

The guys looked at each other. It was Mark who answered.

"To everyone, I think. I have to spy on a woman who works in my office tower. But I'm not telling them anything. I've made Mrs. Towsend sound absolutely boring."

"I'm so glad to hear you say that," said Peter. "I have to spy on one of my customers, and I've also been writing bogus reports."

"What do you mean?" asked Ted, pouring himself another glass of whiskey.

"He's an very nice, old man and I've been delivering his medications. I don't think he realizes that I'm spying on him. He's just so pleased to see me. I also report crap. I don't want any harm to come to him. Pass me the bottle, Ted," said Peter.

After passing the bottle, Ted said, "What about that final statement: a tragedy will occur if we reveal any of this?" Terrified where this talk could lead, Ted wondered if Mark really did extricate all of the listening devices.

In a soft voice, Jack said, "The tragedies must be true. Ted, you remember Annette. She fell apart in gym class because her father suddenly died. You agreed with me the other week that some of the kids were much quieter than usual?"

"We're dead men!" said Gary.

Everyone stared at him. Suddenly, they burst out laughing. They laughed long and hard. The situation they had found themselves in was ridiculous. It felt good to laugh and allow their nervous tension to disperse. As a gesture of complete co-operation, the poker buddies replenished their glasses with whiskey and Mark handed them fresh cigars.

When the happy noise finally petered off, Jack said, "We have to get away from here so we can plan in private how to stop the FSC."

"I agree," said Gary. "Someone has to do something. It might as well be us."

"We should gather our families and meet at my cabin. It's big enough to house everyone. I slipped up there the last weekend and stocked it to the rafters. We can live there until we figure out what to do next," said Jack.

"Sounds good to me," said Ted. "We can't live with these restrictions and expose our families to these nuts."

"We can't trust anyone," Peter added.

"Anyone know what this FSC is? I googled it, but didn't learn much. What does Free Society Council mean?" asked Gary.

"I found the same site," said Mark, "It's all mumbo-jumbo. Didn't understand a damn word."

"Free Society Council," mused Peter. "It means nothing."

"Have you heard anyone talk about it?" Ted looked around at everyone while puffing on his cigar.

Everyone shook their head.

Ted asked, "Anyone find an address for them? Or a phone number? We just mail those damned reports in those plain, white envelopes addressed to an anonymous post office box in D.C."

"Who uses the post office these days? These guys are really bizarre. Why isn't the FSC using email?" asked Mark, exhaling in frustration.

"Maybe that will change," Jack said.

These guys were not the type to give up when things got difficult. They liked a good challenge and never backed down from a fight. And now they had a common enemy, the FSC.

Together, they had defeated many adversaries in the past who tried to make their lives difficult. There was a math professor in university who, for some strange reason, intensely disliked Jack. The guys got together and discredited the man by having it leaked that he plagiarized his latest paper which was true.

There was a student of Jack and Ted's who showed promise as a football player but couldn't afford to buy his own equipment. The guys got together and held a charity dinner where they raised enough money not only for the equipment but to help him afford any college of his choice.

Thrilled with a new challenge, the men considered options of how to stop the FSC. But they had to get away from this dangerous environment and go to a place like Jack's cottage which was isolated. They would pool their knowledge and experience in a place where they could act without being seen.

Peter took a loud slurp of whiskey. They all stopped talking and looked at him.

"We have to do something proactive. We can't be the only ones who want to stop the FSC from taking over. While hiding at Jack's cottage, we must figure something out."

"Fucking right," Gary cried out. "We'll be isolated at the cottage and, from there, we can fight back."

"I'm with you guys but we've got to keep our families safe," said Jack. "We don't want any harm to come to them."

Gary said, "Why don't we use our collective efforts and spy on the FSC?"

The men stared into each other's eyes trying to discern what the others were thinking. They had taken on other challenges together and prevailed, but this was different. There was something dangerous and sinister about the FSC.

Mark knew where to begin. "He's right, but we can't afford to bring any attention to ourselves. So first, I'll go to D.C. and search for that post office box listed on the white envelopes. I'll find out who is taking the mail and where they are taking it to."

"I don't think that's such a good idea," said Ted. "What if you are seen or, even worse, captured?"

"I second that," said Jack.

"You guys worry too much," Gary said dropping his whiskey glass onto the poker table with a thud for effect.

"That's not funny," said Ted.

"Wasn't meant to be funny," said Gary. "Can't you guys make solo decisions?"

"Let's not fight," said Peter. "We have to stick together now."

"I'll be careful and I won't take any chances," said Mark.

Slowly and with some trepidation, the guys agreed to Mark's plan.

"We don't know who or what we're dealing with," warned Jack. "Once you locate that mail's destination, call us. Don't go any further alone."

"Okay. I can do that," said Mark.

"With your findings, we'll discuss together how best to proceed," said Peter.

"Fine. That's settled," said Jack. "Anyone want to play poker?"

No one felt like playing. Their heads were not in it. They stood up and counted their chips. Then they placed them in their personal chip rack. Jack and Ted cleared the table of whiskey glasses and beer bottles while Mark collected all the ashtrays and threw their contents in the garbage. Gary and Peter put the chips away in the cabinet.

The men were prepared to do whatever was necessary. They couldn't allow this craziness to continue. The time to act was now. The FSC had to be stopped. Today was the first step in that direction.

FRIDAY

The next morning, when the poker buddies woke up, they noticed an eerie nervous silence had enveloped the busy streets of the United States. It was as if a thick blanket of solid air had fallen upon the country.

As Gary walked to the radio station, he expected everyone to fill the gray cement sidewalks on their way to work. Now no one spoke, pushed, or jostled for space. Everyone marched slowly along with a quiet determination, staring ahead without looking to either side.

Every once in a while, he heard a snippet of conversation, a few words spoken quietly. Then silence. The only consistent sound heard were shoes hitting bleak pavement. He gazed around at everyone. A tired expression dulled every face.

On the other side of the downtown area, Mark sauntered along the streets on his way to the office. Noticing the drab wear of the other people, he felt out of place in his light blue suit. Gone were bright colors, sexy outfits, and stilettos on the women. They now wore simple, plain dresses. The men wore black, gray, or dark blue suits with neutral-colored ties hoping to blend in. He worried that he stood out. He didn't want to bring unnecessary attention to himself.

It became obvious to Mark that no one wanted to bring attention to themselves, to be noticed or picked out of the crowd. It was as if everyone wished to be invisible. No one raised their eyes to anyone. Each person continued on their own way like horses with blinders.

As Mark and Gary walked in opposite directions, they stared into the streets wondering why no sound came from the traffic. Because of rush hour, the mass of vehicles moved at a snail's pace. Both men noticed there was no honking of horns or yelling by drivers. Drivers simply sat in silence waiting for the traffic to move.

Ted and Jack noticed the other teachers had become suspicious of each other. Everyone acted as if they were hiding something and kept their desks and classrooms locked. No one spoke up at meetings or made any complaints. The men guessed that stress caused by the FSC was changing people. They felt no one could be trusted and the fear of a new person in their lives could only mean catastrophe.

The men watched as mothers walked their children to school. When they passed another mother and child, each lowered their eyes to the children and shook their heads solemnly. Their students spoke to them of family meals held in silence. The children were unable to understand what was happening. They knew something bad had happened, but were too scared to ask what.

The poker buddies made notes of everything. During their poker night, they spent time revealing what they had learned and observed. They noticed one good change. Everyone was afraid to be seen with more money or stuff than their neighbors. Gone were the days that Americans dreamed of being better than the Joneses. The opposite now existed.

Except at schools, the men agreed that the long work days were gone. Everyone spent time spying for two to three hours a day so offices took this into account. Every company including banks were now closing their doors by three p.m. No notices or signs were posted. It was just understood that by three p.m., everyone packed their desks and left work.

Mark mentioned that restaurants were empty. He had gone to dinner with a friend from work and they found themselves alone amongst many empty tables. They had received full attention from their server, who treated them as royalty. He was told by the owner that most restaurants were going bankrupt because no one ate out anymore. The guys guessed that Americans must be terrified to be seen in public.

Over the next few days, the men realized that the FSC had a good hold on the American people. It was obvious that everyone feared the strict rules laid out by the FSC. People really believed that a catastrophe would occur if they did not abide by those rules. Most people didn't question their spying assignments and continued in their difficult path. The poker buddies found themselves caught up in the madness occurring around them.

SUNDAY

At two-thirty p.m. on a bright, sunny Sunday, Mark set off for Washington, D.C. His short flight was scheduled for four p.m. He believed that whoever picked up the mail from Post Office Box 6193 would do so on Monday. He arrived a day early to find a good hiding spot near the post office.

Travelling light, Mark carried one small suitcase and his encased laptop onto the plane. After he settled in his plane seat, he sat back and observed his surroundings. People spoke in whispers and kept their eyes low. Flight attendants were just a little too sweet and helpful.

A young businessman with neatly brushed blond hair, clean-shaven, and wearing an expensive dark navy suit sat down beside Mark. He had a laptop and a briefcase, both of which he placed on the floor underneath his seat.

Mark gazed at the stranger almost willing him to turn and say hello. The wait seemed endless. Finally, the young man acknowledged him. He then turned away and opened his laptop. He angled the screen away from Mark.

A fast learner at spying, Mark turned on the small TV screen on the back of the plane seat in front of him. With his peripheral vision he read the young man's emails. His seat-mate was obviously in retail sales. All the emails were from clients requesting more details about various items for sale.

As the flight took off, the young businessman closed his laptop and took out some papers from his black leather briefcase. He rested his head against the back of the seat and read. Mark decided to take a break from studying him and peered out the oval window in time to watch the plane leave the ground.

When the flight attendant arrived, Mark ordered a beer. His new friend seemed rattled and angry as if he was upset to be disturbed, but ordered a rum and coke.

Mark took the opportunity and turned towards him saying, "Coming or going?"

"Going."

"Yeah, so am I. Hi. I'm Mark Wadley," Mark said holding out his hand.

"Ken. Ken Sommers." Ignoring the gesture, Ken flipped through his business papers.

"Where are you staying? I'm at the Marriott."

"Me too." Ken appeared uninterested in conversation.

"Oh, cool. Want to share a taxi from the airport?" Mark spoke faster than he expected and turned pale when he realized how forward he was being. He worried he had made a mistake.

"Yeah, okay, maybe," Ken replied.

Ken wasn't very friendly but Mark thought that this was an excellent opportunity to see what this guy knew about the FSC, if anything at all. He spied Ken's black briefcase under his seat. He wondered if he could get a chance to look inside. As if by magic, Ken rose from his seat and strolled to the rest room leaving his papers on his seat covered by his laptop.

Usually, people made friendly banter while waiting for the airline toilet but everyone was quiet. People just stood in line, heads bowed, deep in thought. Mark suddenly realized how quiet it was on this flight. There were of course babies crying and children chattering but no adults' voice was raised above a whisper.

Mark bent over and opened Ken's briefcase where he found lots of colored files with addresses on the label. He quickly flicked through them. Then he found what he was searching for: envelopes addressed to P.O. Box 6193, Washington, D.C., the same white envelopes he and his buddies had received. He shut the briefcase and returned it to its place. He found out what he wanted to know. It was obvious Ken spied for the FSC too and this menace happened all over the USA.

As soon as Ken returned, he turned on his laptop leaving Mark to his thoughts. He wondered if there was any question he could ask Ken to find out what he knew without revealing himself. Mark put his head back on the headrest and pondered possible questions but decided to keep it light.

"Is this your first time to D.C.?" Mark said, taking off his headphones.

Sighing, Ken ceased working and politely replied, "No, I visit D.C. often."

"Do you know a good place for a single man to find a good time?" Mark hoped the guy would relax and talk to him.

"Well, there's The Gibson on 14th Street or P.J. Clarke's at 16th and K Streets."

It appeared as if Ken wished to say something more. He slouched in his seat and closed his laptop. He leaned back and looked straight at Mark in the face for the first time.

"What's your story? No prep?"

"All done. Just have to attend," Mark said. "You like the Marriott?"

"It's a good hotel. Off the lobby is an excellent restaurant with the best clam chowder outside of New England."

"Thanks for the info," Mark hoped that the more time he spent with this guy, the better possibility that he would confide in him.

For a few minutes, Ken didn't look at him or say anything. He continued to stare at his feet until he smiled, turned to Ken and said, "Do you ever get tired of the travelling?"

"Sure, but it's part of the job," and the two continued to chat about work for a few more minutes before Ken excused himself and returned to his computer. The rest of the flight was quiet.

Once in his comfortable room at the Marriott, Mark texted Peter that he had arrived. Peter would let the other guys know in some secret way of his own devising. Then he sat down on the king-sized bed with a D.C. map.

The hotel clerk said there was a post office on G Street and Pennsylvania Avenue that had the same area code as the envelopes. He found the area on the map. Mark pulled out his cell phone and searched for the post office's number.

He called and an automated female voice answered. Mark listened to all of the choices then pressed three for directions and hours of operation. The post office was open Monday through Friday from nine in the morning until seven p.m. That would be a long wait, but Mark hoped his mysterious delivery boy would arrive earlier rather than later.

After a few moments deep in thought, he took a shower, changed his clothes, then sat in the hotel bar for a few hours. For spying purposes, Mark chose the small metal table at the far end of the bar so that he could easily observe all the patrons.

Again, he noticed that people seemed more distracted and strained than usual. The few voices took the tone of a low hum as if everyone was scared to speak out loud. There were quite a few people in the bar but most appeared to be singles. He deliberately glanced over the attractive women and tried to connect with a few by staring into their eyes. But no woman would look directly at him. When he did by chance meet with some eyes, they were quickly lowered. It seemed as if every person had put an invisible barrier around themselves.

Just as he was about to leave, Mark noticed Ken Sommers enter the bar alone. Mark raised his hand inviting him to join him at his table. Ken hesitated then smiled. He raised a finger to imply he would be over in a minute. Ken walked straight to the bar, ordered a drink, then carried it over to where Mark sat.

"Night going well?" asked Ken as he sat down. He placed his drink on the metal table in front of him and put his briefcase on the floor beside his feet.

"Fine thanks. How was your meeting?" asked Mark.

"The usual. Lots of noise signalling nothing," Ken said.

Mark smiled recognizing the Shakespearean reference. He was seated with an educated man. He hadn't said anything so profound on the whole plane trip. His defences must be slipping. Ken appeared tired or frustrated by something and Mark wanted to find out if it was because of the FSC.

"How did your meetings go?" Mark asked, taking a sip of his scotch on ice.

Ken smiled with closed eyes. "Got through them. What's wrong with everyone? No one says anything anymore." He sighed loudly.

Mark worked hard to keep his body from jumping and his heart from racing. What he said next was very important. He spoke slowly enunciating every word, "I've noticed that too. Do you know the reason?"

"I have an idea but I don't want to discuss that," said Ken, glancing around the room. "It seems as if everyone's afraid of their shadow."

Mark leaned forward. He wondered how far this Ken guy would go. What should he say next to encourage an exchange of information? He had to know how much this guy knew about the FSC.

"Yes, I agree. Do you know what could be causing this?" Mark asked, as if he had no idea what was happening.

He then saw Ken turn his gaze away from him and stare at the floor. Mark guessed he was trying to figure out if he could be trusted. He probably hadn't spoken to anyone about the package. From what he had discovered about the man, he seemed inquisitive and perhaps the possibility of sharing this part of his life would be irresistible. Or at least he hoped so. Finally, Ken looked up. Like a dam bursting, he revealed everything.

MONDAY

The alarm clock on his bedside table clanged loudly at six-thirty a.m. waking Mark up. He allowed the ringing to bring him back to consciousness. He needed several seconds to remember where he was and why. He dropped his warm feet on the cold, green carpeted floor and slunk into the washroom stepping into the shower.

Once the hot water rushed onto his well-defined body, Mark peed in the shower. His ex-wife had hated that along with a number of other small vices. Mark hadn't thought much about her in a long while. He wondered if she was spying on someone or being spied upon.

He couldn't help thinking about it. Was everyone under the control of the FSC? Mark couldn't imagine where this was headed, but he wasn't about to become a lamb led to the slaughter. He could count on his poker buddies and that was enough for him.

Mark had a quick breakfast in the hotel restaurant then hailed a taxi to the post office at G Street and Pennsylvania Avenue. Upon arriving at the busy intersection, he checked his watch and realized he had arrived fifteen minutes early. He decided to use that time to pick out a good vantage point.

After exiting the taxi, he looked around. He had no trouble locating the post office in question; it had a large clock tower and shared the block with a Bank of America. An array of stores and restaurants completed the area.

A Starbucks stood directly across from the post office and it was the perfect place to wait. He could sit in there by the front window and watch whoever went in and out of the building. But he had to reach the post office box first before the conspirator arrived. He brought a piece of electrical wiring to place on the edge of the box so when someone opened it, the remote would beep.

As soon as the post office opened, Mark entered the grand historic building and immediately searched for Box 6193. When he found the large box, he glanced around. No one was close by, and from the way the clerk was stationed behind the counter, he would not be observed by him.

He noticed a couple of surveillance cameras positioned near the ceiling. Since the box was situated waist-high, he could conceal it while standing directly in front of it. The cameras wouldn't capture his work.

Mark then removed a small piece of gray wire from his coat pocket. It would easily go undetected. Applying some clear glue, Mark adjusted the tiny wire to the big box door. He then brought out a small canister of spray paint and sprayed around the wire. The paint quickly dried to the color of the post office box and the wire lay invisible.

Satisfied with his work, Mark sauntered across the street and into the Starbucks. He bought a Colombian Supreme and took a seat at one of the wooden tables next to large front windows facing Pennsylvania Avenue. Once he adjusted his seat, he had a clear view of the post office's front doors but no one could see him from the outside. He sat back and prepared to wait.

He hoped that the FSC person would arrive soon so he could get back to work. He had asked for a few days using the excuse that he had to do some research. It was easy to get the time off. His boss didn't even blink an eye at his request. In fact, he didn't even look up from his paperwork.

The more Mark thought of it, the more he realized that many people had changed. His boss used to stare at him with those warm, smiling, brown eyes. Now Mark couldn't remember the last time he had looked directly at him. Actually, it had been a long time since anyone had looked him straight in the eye. He made a mental note to speak to the guys about that.

He checked his remote and it was working. His stomach rumbled. He decided it was about time for lunch.

Mark ate at a small classy restaurant recommended by one of the baristas at Starbucks. The eatery was located a block from the intersection. They made a nice Reuben sandwich with potato salad, which he ate with gusto while watching the post office's entrance. A steady stream of individuals came and went.

After lunch, he returned to the Starbucks' table near the window. He picked up another coffee, pulled out a D.C. travel book, then flipped through the pages.

He was about to put the book down when he noticed a familiar image. It was the bank beside the post office. On the next page was a picture of the post office with the clock tower. It was built in the 1890s. The clock tower was 270 feet above street level and offered a 360-degree view of Washington, D.C.

Mark made a few notes but, fearing his notebook would fall into enemy hands, he wrote in a code that only his poker buddies would understand. They used it in college to help them remember all those physics equations. Many nights were spent in memorizing formulas and developing codes. It helped them remember facts for their examinations. They hadn't used this code in years except for the odd joke but he was sure the guys would remember.

A female Barista approached Mark's table and asked if he needed anything. The place was almost empty and Mark guessed she was just looking for something to do.

He gazed up into the woman's face. She was attractive with dyed blond hair and steely blue eyes. Her athletic figure fit well into her brown Starbucks uniform. Leaning over the small table, she tried to read what he had written in his notebook.

"Tourist are ya?" she asked.

"Yes," Mark answered.

"Don't tourists usually visit places, and not just stare at them through a window?" She stood up straight, then cocked her body to show off her good features.

Mark laughed. She had him there. He didn't know how he was going to get out of this one. Then a light bulb flashed in his head, "I'm waiting for a friend."

"I don't think she's coming." She laughed and seemed happy to have someone to chat with. There were only two other patrons in the place.

"How did you know I'm waiting for a woman?" Mark asked, sipping his coffee. He kept his eyes on her over the top of his mug.

"Only a man sits by a window waiting. Women usually give up after thirty minutes." Maggie leaned back and laughed at her own joke.

Mark decided to play her game because she looked at him straight in the eye. He winked and smiled. "Well, to tell you the truth, I don't know when she's coming. I just know that sometime today she'll go into that post office."

"Boy, are you in love." Maggie sounded a little jealous.

"No, not in love. Let's just say I have to speak with her."

"You've got a kid together?"

It was Mark's turn to laugh. "No kids. I promise you," and flashed her the boy-scout salute.

"Well, I'm Maggie Myers. If you need anything, just ask." She returned to her station behind the glass counter.

Mark knew most women were attracted to him, but for some strange reason everything went sour after a few months. The problem was that women wanted to change him and he couldn't stand that. When they asked to move in with him, he ran.

In the past, he had let a couple of women move in but they would rearrange his house. It drove him crazy. Maybe this Maggie would be different and possibly of some use. Her demeanor was friendly and open, the opposite of what he had seen lately with most people. She obviously wasn't as yet an FSC victim.

Watching Maggie serve two older gentlemen, Mark bet all his chips that she flirted with both of them. She was his type: athletic, blond, blue eyes and a ready smile. He would keep an eye on this one. He smiled thinking she might be useful in more than one way.

* * *

Earlier that day, Ted woke up sweating. He couldn't remember what he had dreamed, but it caused his heart to race. They were crazy to let Mark go on his own. He had received Jack's text message at around eleven p.m. with just two words: *full house*, meaning that Mark had found the post office and was prepared to wait on Monday. Ted worried that the longer Mark had to wait, the more dangerous it could become for him.

Then his tired eyes rested on his sleeping wife. The guys had decided not to involve their wives in their D.C. games. There would be time enough to tell them.

Dressing in a white t-shirt and black gym shorts, Ted quietly stepped into the family's den. He removed a few books from the shelves revealing a video machine. Jack suggested they all put up surveillance cameras.

Ted ejected the disc from the machine and replaced it with a blank one. He then inserted the disc into his laptop. Every morning, he woke up early to watch the show.

In the beginning, he had enjoyed watching the kids at play until he noticed a blue Ford Escort parked across the street one house down. The blue vehicle arrived every day at approximately three-thirty p.m., when Susan returned home after picking up their kids from school. The vehicle remained until after he returned from work. It left every day at seven p.m.

It was difficult to avoid staring at the Ford Escort when he returned home from work. He sometimes stayed in his car a few extra minutes pretending to look for something. He moved his rear-view mirror to get a good view of the Escort. There was one occupant.

After fastening a camera onto the light post, Ted got a clearer image of the spy. He fast-forwarded through the disc until the Escort arrived. He then brought up the lamp-post camera. He zoomed in until he could obtain a clear view of the occupant. He dropped back in his chair in shock. He couldn't believe it but the spy was Marion, a cashier who worked at the local Walmart.

Susan did all the family's shopping at that Walmart. She and Marion had been friends for years. Susan had even invited Marion to their house last year for a big Independence Day barbeque.

Ted couldn't fault Marion. She was just following orders. He would ask Susan at breakfast whether she had noticed any change in Marion. He considered whether or not to approach Marion. However, he wasn't sure whether she could be counted on not to report their conversation to the FSC. Her car was most certainly bugged. He would speak to Jack before doing anything further.

* * *

Someone dropped a coffee cup. Mark heard the mug shatter. The sudden sharp noise took his attention away from the front window. When he looked back to the street, he noticed two people going into the post office. One was an older woman in a green dress carrying a package. The other was a well-dressed man in a black business suit carrying a large black briefcase similar to those used by attorneys.

As the young man came up behind the old woman, he opened the door for her. The woman smiled at the man and said something. Mark made a silent note of the man. The man's short blond hair stood straight up probably from too much gel. He wore dark sunglasses though the sun wasn't very bright.

His suspicions heightened, Mark packed up his belongings preparing for a quick exit. He waited for the remote to beep. When organized, he put his briefcase on the chair and noted the time in his notebook. Suddenly, his small remote began to beep. He turned it off, threw it is his pocket, and took up position outside the coffee shop closer to the curb.

A young, black man with a child came out of the post office. A few minutes later, the older woman in the green dress exited without a package. Then, an old man.

Finally, after what seemed like an hour, the blond man with the black briefcase left the post office. He opened up the front doors with a big push using the side of his body and headed down the stairs. His eyes flickered taking in everything around him. He crossed G Street and opened the door to a silver SUV parked at the curb. Mark ran into the street and flagged down the first taxicab. Just as the cabbie asked for the destination, the silver SUV pulled out into traffic.

"Follow that car," Mark instructed.

"Okay, your dime," replied the driver.

He drove one car length behind the intended target. Mark rested his arms on the clear glass separating him from the cabbie and glared at the silver vehicle. He wasn't about to lose this guy.

The taxi followed the silver SUV west on Pennsylvania until they reached 21st Street. They imitated the SUV's left turn. He then took a right on Virginia and the cabbie pointed out the Watergate office complex to Mark who didn't seem too interested in the scenery.

The blond man took a right on I-66 and up the GW Parkway taking the taxi past the Kennedy Center. They followed the silver SUV onto the Theodore Roosevelt Bridge leading to an area near D.C. called Bethesda, one of the more affluent neighborhoods.

After the pleasant but long tour of the city, the blond man turned into an enormous, metal-gated paved driveway bordered by thick hedges. No clear view of the grounds or house was available from the road.

"Pull up here," said Mark, gesturing just beyond the metal gates where the silver SUV had turned. Mark pulled his hood over his head and adjusted his sunglasses.

"Can you wait a sec?" Mark said.

"Sure buddy," replied the cabbie.

Mark opened the rear car door. Surveillance cameras covered the gate and massive hedge, but his curiosity had the better of him. He planted himself on the sidewalk then slowly walked past the metal-gated driveway. Mark couldn't see through or over the large green hedges that grew on either side of the gate.

Gathering his courage, he ran up to the gate. There was a digital keypad at the side on a metal stand just before the gate. As he glanced through the iron gate, he could distinguish a large building at the end of a curved driveway. Using his cell phone, he took a few pictures then ran back to the cab and jumped in.

Mark said, "Thanks, pal. Please take me to the Marriott."

The taxi driver, a man in his early fifties, turned around and looked Mark straight into his eyes. He was a typical Italian immigrant with black hair and deep brown eyes. Though an average frame, he was a little on the pudgy side.

"Are you spying on someone or what?" he asked after pulling out into traffic.

Shocked by these words, Mark reviewed his actions and realized that was exactly what it would look like he was doing.

"It's okay. I've had lots of people use my cab to spy on someone. Don't understand why everyone is suddenly spying but it's good money."

Mark breathed slowly and deeply. "Are there a lot of people spying these days?"

"Actually," said the driver, "Now that I think about it, I'm on the hunt with several people every day. I usually keep quiet and just follow their instructions. Never been out this way before. By the way, I'm Tony."

"Hi Tony. I'm Mark. Nice to meet you. Do you mind explaining a little bit about what you've been doing for these people?"

Obviously Tony had not been recruited by the FSC and he seemed like an open and honest man. What he said could be very valuable to the guys. Mark pulled out his notepad and sat back.

Tony breathed deeply, then let it all pour out. Mark relaxed and listened to Tony and his stories. It was obvious that Tony had little difficulty driving and that he was taking the long route to the hotel. He talked during the whole ride.

"Most of the jobs are like yours: following someone. But usually they want to watch a place for a while. That's when it really gets pricey. I like those ones."

"Does this happen much?"

"It's been happening a lot lately. I first thought people were government but nah they're just like you and me. Most of them shake so bad, I turn up the heat thinking they're cold. Now I know they are just freaking out. I think everyone's gone crazy."

Everyone has gone crazy, thought Mark. This guy was right. Tony obviously hadn't heard about the FSC or he wouldn't be talking so casually about spying.

Mark needed to talk to his friends. He looked at Tony's cab identification and wrote down his last name and taxi number.

"Listen Tony, I'm in a bit of a pickle. I can't tell you much about what I'm doing now, but I'm sure to be back in D.C. Could I have your cell? You're just the man I need."

"Thanks buddy. Sure you can trust me. I'd be glad to help. Just ask." He turned, looked Mark right in the eye, then added, "Can you give me a clue? I hate being left out of the loop."

"I think someone is manipulating Americans to spy for them. It's all over the U.S.A. I'm from Boston and some friends and I have been pressured into spying. I came here to try and find out who's doing this."

Turning the rear-view mirror, Tony said, "That silver SUV is doing this?"

Leaning back into the seat so Tony could see him better, Mark said, "Who knows? It may be him or he may just work for someone. You've never received a package from the FSC?"

Tony paused for a second, which was a long time for him, then said, "No, can't say that I have."

"Here's my card," said Mark, handing it over through a hole in the dividing glass.

Just after accepting the card, Tony pulled up in front of the Marriott.

After Mark exited the vehicle, he said, "If you ever do hear from them, call me. Be careful Tony."

"Thanks man," Tony said, noticing the large tip. "Good luck."

Mark patted the front right fender of the cab and then waved goodbye to Tony. He walked into the Marriott and headed towards the hotel bar. When the bartender came by, Mark ordered a straight scotch.

After the first big sip, he turned around and surveyed his surroundings. It was late afternoon and the crowd seemed to encompass mostly business people, though there were a few couples. A few single people were interspersed around the room. They just stared into their glasses. Mark's green eyes rested on two well-dressed, classy women at a table to his left.

Knowing there was nothing more he could do until he talked with the guys and his flight wasn't leaving until the next morning, he had a free night. *Might as well get laid,* he thought. He rose from the stool and walked directly up to the table with the two attractive women figuring he'd get lucky with at least one of them. He smiled seductively hoping for a threesome.

THURSDAY

The green felt poker table in Mark's home was set up. The chip trays were in their correct positions in front of the chairs and the Dominican cigars were on the side table along with a bottle of whiskey. The playing cards were displayed in a fan showing all four suits. The guys would be arriving soon.

Mark rested uncomfortably in front of a blank television wondering what they were going to do next in their pursuit of the FSC. As expected, he had been submitting the spy reports every week but, as agreed to with the guys, he wrote the most banal and unassuming information. None of the men wished to cause a ripple in the ocean of the FSC. They didn't want to bring any attention to themselves.

Taking out his notebook, Mark flipped through the few pages of notes to refresh his memory. Smiling, he thought of Maggie as he re-read his comments about her. She was definitely an unexpected angle in this whole affair. Something about her made him wonder if they would meet again. He would like that.

The poker buddies had decided that Mark would text Peter the message, *the nuts*, as soon as he returned to his hotel room the previous Monday night. The message would imply he was safe in the hotel and that the mission was a success. He did feel a little guilty for messaging him so late.

A knock at the front door awakened him out of his revelries. He peeked at his watch: seven-thirty. Someone was early.

Mark found Peter standing on his front stoop. He was dressed in a plain, blue suit with a slightly crumpled light blue shirt. His blue-striped tie was slightly askew. Smiling nervously, Peter held up a case of beer.

"I thought we could use this," Peter said as he walked straight past Mark and into the kitchen.

If Peter brought beer something was wrong. He rarely bought alcohol because he didn't drink much. Usually, one glass of whiskey was enough for him.

Peter plopped the heavy box on the marble counter, then stepped aside to allow Mark to open the refrigerator door.

"Did you have to message me so late? I was frantic waiting for your text," Peter said.

"Sorry, got side-tracked." A sly smile crept across Mark's handsome face.

Peter knew he meant a woman. It was a reason but not a good one.

"I messaged the other guys but they didn't read it until the morning. Don't scare us like that again," said Peter, placing the beer case in the fridge.

"I'm sorry. Have you talked to anyone?" asked Mark closing the fridge door.

"Gary, Anne, and Renee came over Sunday for dinner, but Gary and I were unable to speak privately. How did it go?"

"Mainly held out in Starbucks and enjoyed the view."

Both men enjoyed a lighthearted snicker knowing Mark didn't mean just the post office.

Another loud knock was heard. Jack and Ted opened the unlocked front door and entered Mark's house. Both were dressed casually in golf shirts and jeans.

They nodded a silent greeting as they made their way into Mark's living room. Both Ted and Jack touched Mark lightly on his shoulder as they walked past him.

"Hey! Wait for me," Gary shouted as he crossed the threshold.

One by one they all sat down in their usual places at the poker table. Mark picked up the cards and began shuffling. Everyone sat in silence as Mark dealt the cards face up to see who would draw the first jack and therefore be the first to deal. A jack of clubs landed in front of Gary.

Mark retrieved the cards and passed them to Gary who said, "We're really going to play? Aren't you going to tell us what happened?"

"Yeah," Jack said. "Spill the beans."

"Yes, we all want to know what happened," agreed Ted.

While all the guys nodded their heads in assent, Mark pulled out his notebook and laid it on the poker table. With a deep breath, he detailed his interesting adventure. He smiled proudly when he revealed that the thin wire and remote had achieved their purpose. That had been a group suggestion.

He then described the silver SUV, the blond man, and his destination. He also relayed his long and detailed conversation with Tony, the taxicab driver.

"I should return to that mansion and set up surveillance cameras in those hedges," Ted said, perusing the pictures of the area around the ornate metal gate.

"No, that's too dangerous," said Peter, leaving the table to grab beers for everyone.

"It's worth a chance. I've become quite adept with video cameras. Found my spy," said Ted with a big smile on his face.

"How?" said the guys almost in unison.

"I set up four cameras on lamp posts around my house. I've been reviewing the tapes every morning," said Ted. "I've discovered that my spy is a Walmart cashier."

"You recognized her?" asked Gary.

"Yes. Do you think I should approach her?" Ted asked, accepting a beer from Peter.

"That's tricky," Peter answered. "Are you sure you can trust her? I don't think you should chance it."

"I agree. We need additional information about the FSC before we begin prying into our spies," said Jack, opening his beer and taking a big gulp.

"That's fine," replied Ted. "I'll fly to D.C. this weekend and set up those cameras."

"I think you're crazy," Gary blurted out.

"You're taking a big chance," said Jack.

"I agree," said Peter, leaning over to the cabinet. He drew a cigar out of the small wooden box resting near the edge of the cherry wood cabinet.

"Yes, I'm taking a chance but this is the logical next step in the process," said Ted. "I'll take a cigar."

Peter handed out cigars to each of the guys while Jack squirmed in his chair. Usually, he was on Ted's side during an argument, but he agreed with the majority this time. On the other hand, this was the next important step in their progression in determining who the FSC was.

"You're right, Gary, but Ted, you should think twice about this. Are you sure you want to go to D.C.?" asked Jack, lighting his cigar.

"Yes, I am. Don't worry. I'll be fine. Are you sure we can trust this taxi driver?" Ted asked Mark.

"Definitely sure. He's verbose, but comprehends the importance of silence," said Mark raising his beer.

"Good. Let's go book a ticket on your computer. Back in a sec guys," said Ted, putting down his beer.

Ted and Mark moved into Mark's office. Mark wiggled the mouse on the desk and his computer came alive. He scrolled through his favorites until he found the United Airline's website.

"Okay. What time do you want to leave?" asked Mark.

"That seven a.m. flight on Saturday with a return the same day," replied Ted.

"Done. How about a four p.m. return? That should give you enough time, right?"

"Right. That's great. Thanks Mark," said Ted, leaning back in the comfortable chair across the table from Mark.

The website asked for Ted's credit card number. Ted pulled out his Visa and read out the number. Once they had completed their work, Mark printed out Ted's itinerary and plane tickets. Ted glanced over it, then stuffed the papers into his jean pocket.

When Ted and Mark returned, Gary readied the cards to deal. Once they were handed out, it was Ted's turn to bet. He threw down a few chips into the space just in front of him.

The other guys stared at Ted and chuckled. Ted rarely bet so much at the first position of the poker table. He was obviously bluffing, a rarity for Ted. Their little mission had given them all an extra boost of confidence.

Peter bet next. Smiling widely while attempting to keep a straight face, he threw in his chips and called Ted's bet. The guys all stopped, looked at each other, and started laughing letting go some of the nervous tension.

Before making a decision, Jack turned to Ted and said, "Message me the moment you get to the airport, okay?"

"Yes, mother. I'll text immediately."

That broke them up again and they all laughed. Everyone joked that Ted and Jack were really a married couple.

When the noise died down, Peter left his chair and said, "Who wants another beer?"

Four hands shot up into the air. Peter walked into the kitchen and retrieved five bottles.

As they twisted off the caps, there was a communal sigh of relief. They all had a deep first gulp. Then they put their beers into the appropriate cup holders on the poker table so that the green felt would not be ruined.

"The bet is yours, Jack," said Mark who had just folded.

Jack threw the required number of chips into the pot. Gary tossed in the same. The flop was a jack of hearts, a jack of diamonds, and a four of hearts.

After a few minutes, Ted counted out some chips and made his bet.

When it was Peter's turn, he paused for a few minutes then pushed some chips into the kitty.

Gary dealt the turn card and placed it on the table beside the flop. It was the eight of hearts, bringing a potential flush to the board. Ted checked but Peter threw in some chips. Ted called. The rest folded.

Dealing the river card, Gary turned up the six of hearts. Ted bet but Jack raised. Peter slyly glanced at Jack and, without looking at his chips, he called Jack's raise.

Once all the chips were in, they turned over their cards. Peter had the king of hearts and so had a flush but Jack had pocket fours, which gave him a full house.

Jack chuckled then reached over to draw in the accumulated poker chips towards his stockpile. Gary handed the cards to Mark.

Shuffling the deck a little longer than necessary, Mark said, "I met a woman at the Starbucks."

The guys raised their eyebrows and smiled knowingly at Mark. Women were always drawn to him.

"Not that kind of meeting," he replied with a snicker. "She's a Barista and her name is Maggie."

"Has she been compromised?" said Jack.

"No, I don't think so," said Mark. He thought about how she had looked him straight in the eye and how she had talked to him so freely. "She didn't seem to know about the FSC."

"Could we trust her?" asked Gary, butting out his cigar.

"Possibly. She could keep a lookout on the post office and see how often that blond guy goes in," said Mark.

"Good idea," agreed Jack. "Hey Ted, why don't you look her up when you're there?"

"That wouldn't be a problem."

After dealing the cards, Mark said, "Tell her I was the one whose girlfriend never showed up. I'm sure that stuck in her mind because that's what she thought I was doing there. I didn't want to contradict her."

Peter bet, then Jack raised. Ted folded. Peter called while Gary and Mark folded. The flop came nine of clubs, six of hearts, seven of spades. Jack threw in a few chips. Peter called.

The turn revealed the queen of diamonds. Peter bet a few more chips. Jack raised. The river showed a king of spades. Peter bet and Jack called.

Then the men flipped over their cards. Jack had a ten and jack showing the nut straight. He grabbed the chips and handed his cards to Peter whose turn it was to deal.

Peter shuffled a little roughly. That was the second hand in a row he had lost to Jack. He was now the short stack at the table.

"I'm going to deal myself a doozy," said Peter.

While Peter dealt, Gary rose and collected all the empty beer bottles. He whipped into the kitchen and replaced the empties with cold ones from the refrigerator.

The men played for another hour, then decided to pack it in. They all seemed a little distracted. At the door, they wished Ted good luck and sauntered out into the night.

On all their minds was Ted's mission. Would he be noticed? Would he have any problems setting up the cameras? What he was doing was potentially very dangerous.

SATURDAY

First thing in the morning, Ted phoned Tony, the D.C. taxi driver, and arranged to be picked up at the airport. They would travel to the same address where Mark had gone. Tony asked no questions and Ted made no comments.

While flying, Ted reviewed Mark's photographs and notes. Once he had everything in order, his thoughts turned to the lie he had told Susan. He'd said that he needed to complete some work at school and he would be gone all day.

He had never lied to her before. They believed in honesty and complete trust but he didn't want to worry her. He would eventually tell her everything after his adventure. It was dangerous but, with every fiber of his being, he knew it was the right thing to do.

When Ted left the busy Dulles airport, he walked to the end of the pick-up area where a taxi waited. Ted poked his head into the open window and said, "Are you Tony?"

"Yup. You Ted?" said Tony looking up from a newspaper.

"Yup," said Ted, jumping into the backseat.

Tony turned around and gave Ted a big wide smile. Then he said, "You'll be wanting to go where Mark went?"

Ted nodded in the affirmative.

"Okay. It's a bit of a drive from here, but I've found a short cut. Sit back and relax."

And that's just what Ted did. He rested his head against the back of the seat, barely registering the various buildings they passed. Ted knew Tony's curiosity was killing him but he wasn't in the mood to talk.

When they reached a residential area, Ted began to pay attention. After a few more turns, the taxi followed a long road of gated mansions spaced widely apart. Tony drove past a few and stopped just beyond one mansion's driveway. Ted stared at the address: 320 Sycamore Avenue. This was the place.

Ted said, "I have to set up some equipment. Can you wait about ten minutes?"

"No problem, pal," and Tony picked up the newspaper. Though he seemed to be reading, Ted could feel the cabbie's eyes on the back of his head.

After opening his suitcase on the sidewalk, Ted scanned the area and saw no one around. He grabbed the cameras and pliers then stuck the wires up his sleeves like he was hiding cards. Once all was ready, he made his way over to the hedge.

Grabbing a branch, Ted attached a small green-colored camera using the green wires up his sleeve. Once it was fixed and hidden, he selected three more branches and placed cameras on each of them. These cameras would provide a good view of whomever entered or exited the driveway.

Once he was satisfied with the job, he gathered up his tools and threw them in the black suitcase.

Jumping back into the cab, Ted shouted at Tony, "Let's get out of here."

Tony dropped the newspaper at his side and immediately started the taxi. He stepped on the accelerator and they shot down the empty street.

Once they were a distance from the mansion, Ted breathed a huge sigh of relief. In a casual tone, he gave Tony the address of the Starbucks where Mark's new friend Maggie worked. But coffee? What he really needed was a straight scotch.

Ted could tell the cabbie was dying to talk since he could see him glancing at him through the rear-view mirror every few moments.

"Are you planning to tell anyone about where we were or what I did?" Ted said staring straight into the mirror.

Tony shook his head. "No pal. I see nothing. I know nothing," he said imitating Sergeant Schultz from *Hogan's Heroes*.

"Thanks." Ted laughed and leaned back in the seat.

"But if you want to tell me about it, I'd appreciate it. I know how to keep my mouth shut." He glanced into his side mirror and changed lanes.

Ted liked this guy. "My friends and I are spying on the FSC."

"Mark told me about the FSC, but I haven't received a package from them yet. I do get a lot of fares who spy on someone."

"Do these people tell you anything?" He straightened his back and placed his hands on the divider.

"Nah. They're just loaded down with notebooks and cameras. They give me an address, and we sit in front of a building for a while. Mark was the same so I thought he was doing the same thing. I keep my nose out of it, but he was the first one to tell me anything." He flipped on his signal light and turned right.

"Be very careful revealing what you know. Don't trust anyone!" Ted paused to let that last statement sink in. "Mark said you'd be willing to help us."

"Sure, pal. What do you want?"

"Would you be willing to go out to that mansion again?" He sat with his face up against the glass.

"Okay. And do what?" He swore under his breath as he was cut off by another taxi.

"Would you check out the place once or twice a week for any changes? Let us know if you see anything different."

"Sure, but you don't expect me to do this out of the goodness of my heart? You seem like nice guys but I've got bills to pay."

Ted glanced at the fare machine: $70.25. Playing with some figures in his head, Ted said, "How's two hundred dollars?"

That would be forty dollars from each of the guys. They could easily come up with that. Ted figured it was a fair amount and Tony agreed.

"Mark didn't say much but that you guys are poker buddies?"

"That's true. We've been playing cards together since college."

"Wow that's incredible. I've got a few friends from the old neighborhood still in my life but I don't know if I could trust them now. Some have changed, especially when they married." Tony let out a huge laugh.

"Mark's the only one of our group not married. Our wives get along quite well, but I know what you mean about changing." Ted and Tony both gave a knowing laugh.

"We used to live such easy-going lives with no real worries. Ever since the FSC came into existence, we've got something to stress over and bags are appearing under everyone's eyes," said Ted.

"Yes, I've noticed the same thing. This is no way to live."

When they arrived outside the Starbucks, Ted left the cab with his now empty suitcase. He leaned over to grab Tony's offered hand.

"Deal's a deal?" Tony said as their hands shook.

"Yup. Here you go," Ted said as he handed over three hundred dollars in cash: one hundred for today and two hundred in lieu of future help.

Ted thanked Tony again then walked into the café. He examined the empty Starbucks restaurant from the front door.

There were two attractive women working behind the counter. He recognized Maggie immediately from

Mark's description. Ted chucked to himself about how well Mark knew women.

Maggie's blond hair was tied back revealing large hoop earrings that beautifully showed off her long neck. She was dressed in the standard, neatly pressed, Starbucks' uniform. He made his way to the counter where Maggie was standing.

Looking Ted over, Maggie listened while he ordered a mocha latte. Ted hoped the sugar would urge him along. He then asked her to bring it over to his table. Maggie's bright blue eyes sparkled yes.

He smiled in return and left to find a private table close to the window. He wanted to check out the post office. When Maggie arrived with his coffee, he introduced himself as Mark's friend and said that he would appreciate it if they could talk for a few minutes.

"Let me take care of those two over there, and then I can sit with you," said Maggie.

Ted watched her work. When she finished, she sat down across from him. He could feel her eyes sizing him up. Then her eyes rested on his wedding band.

"You're married?" Maggie asked nodding at the ring.

Ted lifted up his left hand, wiggled his fingers, and smiled in the affirmative.

"Is Mark?"

"Nope."

Maggie's smile brightened and said, "Nice. Is he coming back?"

Ted laughed. Mark had done it again. He was blissfully unaware of how easily women fell in love with him. Whenever they went out, Ted noticed how women's eyes followed Mark. The women who met him were ready to have his baby after hello.

Ted peered again at Maggie and realized she was definitely Mark's type. He considered whether to tell her that Mark might not be back but thought better of it. "I don't know for sure or when, but there is always a possibility," Ted finally said.

After adjusting the cup of latte on the small table to a more convenient place, he then gazed up into Maggie's stunning blue eyes and said, "Can we talk seriously for a moment?"

"Sure love," replied Maggie.

Ted pulled out Mark's black, square beeper, which was still connected to the FSC's post office box. He put it on the metal table.

"Can you tell us how often this beeper goes off and when? Could you keep a journal for us?" Ted passed the device to her.

Raising her eyebrows and widening her eyes, she said, "Sure, but why do you want me to do that?"

"I need to know how often a box is opened in the post office across the street."

"Do you want me to find out who gets the mail?"

"No, thanks. We know who picks it up. We just need to know how often," said Ted.

The guys could be putting this woman's life in harm's way if the blond man noticed her. But if she could see him from the café window and not show herself to the man, it could possibly work.

Ted carefully explained to Maggie how the small beeper worked and about the blond man in the silver SUV. He asked her to check at what time he opened the mailbox. Under no condition was she to approach the blond man or allow him to see her watching him. Maggie nodded her head at each statement and smiled. She promised to keep a journal.

Suddenly, Ted thought of a good idea. "I'll have Mark call you to check up on your progress okay?"

Ted knew her answer even before she blushed. She seemed excited about having another chance with Mark. He watched her flatten out her skirt on her legs, erasing the crumpled parts.

Changing the subject, Ted said, "Have you ever received a brown, paper package from the FSC?"

"FSC? No. Never heard of them. Why would they send me a package?" Maggie asked.

Relieved she hadn't been corrupted as of yet, Ted had only more warnings for her. "If you ever do, let us know right away. The FSC is very dangerous. Have you noticed anything unusual about people these days?"

Maggie suddenly shuddered, "Now that you mention it, yes I have. Everyone seems a little more distracted these days. No one smiles anymore. I've wondered what was going on. Are you saying someone is causing this?"

"Yes, the FSC," explained Ted. "For some reason, the FSC wants everyone to spy on someone and then report our findings to them."

"Have you received that parcel?" asked Maggie.

"I received my mission a few months ago. I have to spy on a co-worker, but I report crap and it doesn't seem to matter. We don't know who is reading this stuff or what it all means. All we know is that post office across the street is where our reports go."

Maggie sat back in her metal chair and breathed deeply a couple of times. She nervously glanced around the shop and took in the situation. She wasn't needed at the counter. June was talking on the phone. She looked back at Ted.

"Okay. I'll see what I can do. Do you want any more coffee?" Maggie asked.

"No, thanks. I've got to go. Here's my card. Please don't hesitate to call if something happens. I don't want to scare you, but this is dangerous business."

Maggie smiled and promised to do her best. Ted wondered if she was taking him that seriously but it was a head's up situation. If she thought she could have another opportunity with Mark, it could be well worth it for her.

As she rose from the small table, Ted followed suit. They moved towards each other and shook hands. Ted waved as he exited through the front door.

Ted hailed a taxi to the airport. His flight was due to leave in an hour and he was still in need of a strong drink. So Ted headed to the airport bar as soon as he had passed through the ticket counter and security.

He settled himself and ordered a straight scotch. After he downed a couple of deep sips, he pulled out his cell phone and texted Jack the message *trips*, their code that he had accomplished all three missions. He then perused the bar's small menu as his stomach growled. He chose some hot wings then centered his attention on his scotch.

When Ted arrived home, he greeted his family then they enjoyed a good meal. After dinner, the children were sent to their bedrooms to finish their homework and Ted ran into his study. After firing up his computer, he clicked onto to his surveillance programs.

He linked to the cameras in the hedges at 320 Sycamore Avenue. He fast-forwarded until a vehicle came into view then took notes of the type of car, license plate, and number of occupants. Four cars passed through those gates.

Every day, Ted found a few minutes to check out the surveillance cameras. He printed the pictures of every vehicle that came into view of their cameras.

None of the vehicles were of much interest except one which was a limo. Who was in that limo and what connection did he have to the FSC?

THURSDAY

As usual, the five buddies sat in their regular seats at Mark's poker table, but there was no pretense of playing cards. The cards remained in the box. They had involved themselves in a much bigger game now with much higher stakes. As they held their cigars, they sipped whiskey.

They were all smiling; it had been a while since they had worked collectively to accomplish something. Not since the days when they played practical jokes on each other and unsuspecting college friends.

There were the exploding film containers that scared most people causing them to fall down and run away screaming. The typical physics tricks with water bottles and toothpicks in forks and spoons suspended on the rims of glasses. Even though most of these tricks were done to impress women, this was a group of guys who knew how to laugh and have fun.

Leaning back in his chair, Gary said, "So Ted, what have you got?"

Placing his briefcase on the poker table, Ted opened it with a squeak and explained what he had discovered.

"I'm pretty sure I wasn't seen nor have they found the cameras. We've been lucky so far. Seven assorted cars and trucks have come and gone from that gate.

"One was the blond guy in that silver SUV. He obviously lives in the mansion. Every day at precisely one p.m., he leaves the mansion and returns at precisely two-thirty p.m. I have his license plate number, as I do with all the other cars. Gary, can you hack into the DMV?"

Gary, their resident computer geek, nodded. Ted tossed him a piece of paper with a list of the license plates.

Ted continued, "There was also a black stretch limo. The driver had no distinguishing features. I couldn't see who was sitting in the back. Then a green Jaguar appeared.

"The fourth vehicle was a black Nissan Sonata driven by an older man. He doesn't live in the mansion. He arrives two to three afternoons a week and stays until early evening. The last car is a blue Hyundai Accent driven by a woman who has two female passengers. They arrive every day at nine-thirty a.m. and leave around seven p.m."

"What about the other two vehicles?" asked Jack.

"One was a truck from a local landscaping company. I checked them out. They're legit. The other was a delivery truck from Walgreens. It arrived every Wednesday around two in the afternoon. It remained for about twenty minutes."

Suddenly Jack said, "That's our way in."

All the guys looked at him in shock.

"One of us should take the place of the Walgreens driver and scope out the mansion."

"Ha," laughed Ted. "You've been watching too many movies."

"I'm serious!" Jack said, almost shouting.

Rising from his chair, Jack walked around the poker table and up to the wooden cabinet along the far wall. He picked up a bottle of scotch and refilled everyone's glass.

"I want to see what's in that place. Peter, can you prepare a fast sedative to knock out the driver of the delivery truck? I'll take his place and have a quick look around."

"Are you nuts?" Gary scoffed. "You're coming out betting crazy."

"Possibly, but if Jack wants to chance it, he should go for it," said Mark who was also very interested to know what was going on inside that mansion.

"No," said Ted. "You can't."

The men fell silent. Each considered whether they would have the courage to do what Jack implied.

"Hey," Mark said. "What about this? I'll call Tony and ask him to follow that Walgreens truck and find out its route."

"Good idea," said Jack as he slowly blew cigar smoke into the air.

Ted considered options then said, "Tony can take you to the stop before the mansion."

Carrying on with the idea, Peter said, "Once Tony leaves you, you put the driver to sleep. I can give you a sedative."

"That's great. You can leave the truck in the Walgreens parking lot. The driver will wake up not knowing what happened," said Mark.

"We could plan for it, say, next week," said Jack. "That should give Tony enough time to get the route."

"Are you nuts?" Gary blurted out, dropping his glass on the table. "Do you think this is a movie where the good guys always come out on top? This is real life and very dangerous."

"C'mon guys. I need a little excitement in my life, and we're doing the right thing. I just know it. Someone has to expose the FSC," said Jack.

The guys puffed their cigars and took sips of whiskey while thinking of what to say.

"Well, don't take any chances," said Ted.

"I'll be fine, Mother. Peter, when can you give me that sedative?" asked Jack.

"Come over tomorrow after school and I'll set you up with a syringe," said Peter. "You want me to go with you?"

Jack took a sip of whiskey then said, "Thanks, but no. I'll be less conspicuous if I go alone."

"Why don't you and the family come over for dinner Saturday night? I'll give you what I've found out about those other cars going into the mansion," said Gary.

"Sounds good to me. Let's play a few hands," said Jack, as he grabbed the cards from the table and began shuffling.

They played for over an hour. Every so often, one of the guys would look questioningly at Jack.

Each time, Jack shouted, "I'll be fine!" and they continued playing.

With final assurances from Jack, the guys felt excited and nervous when they left Mark's house. Jack and Ted got into Jack's car and sped off towards home.

Ted kept looking at Jack with his peripheral vision while pretending to stare out the front window. Unable to stand the silence, he said, "I'll drive you to the airport. Call me when you have the flight and time of arrival."

"Thanks," said Jack. "That would be great. I'm sure I'll get in just after dinner. Listen. If anything happens . . . " Jack let his voice trail off.

"Don't worry. Just try and find out as much as possible in that short time. You're in and out," Ted smiled.

Jack laughed. Ted could always calm him. What he planned was dangerous, but this was the obvious next step in discovering the truth.

SATURDAY NIGHT

Five square pieces of white bond paper rested in a blank manila envelope in Gary's wall safe. What he possessed was dangerous and he had to keep it hidden.

He kept the wooden blinds closed and had two different firewalls and a security code on his computer. He wished anyone luck who tried to hack in. To be extra careful though, he had deleted any record that his computer had made of his research into the DMV and online sites.

When Jack and his family arrived, the four children immediately ran into the backyard. Laura joined Anne in the kitchen. Gary maneuvered Jack into his office where he locked the door. He walked to the opposite wall and unlocked the safe. Gary pulled out the brown envelope and tossed it onto the desk in front of Jack.

The first DMV report described Angela Barrett. She was five-feet-eight inches tall with blond hair and brown eyes, weighing 125 pounds. She had one infraction for speeding a couple of years ago but otherwise had a clean report.

Gary Googled her but there was nothing about where she had lived or worked three years ago. She was now employed with a housekeeping company.

Angela was single and Peter took a good look at her photo, not a bad looking woman even for a driver's license photo. Her file held nothing else of interest.

Jack flipped to the next page and saw the Walgreens delivery truck. He placed that page aside from the others then noticed Gary preparing glasses of brandy. They never drank brandy unless it was a special occasion.

Jack stuck his hand in the air as if to ask a question, but all Gary said was "Read on."

The black limousine was owned by one Harold Hartley. The paper gave his address as 320 Sycamore Avenue, Washington, D.C. He was tall and commanding at six-foot-five-inches with gray hair and striking blue eyes. His photo showed him to be a man who probably never smiled. He was registered as a scientist for the Roosevelt Institute, a D.C. think tank.

That was interesting. He was a scientist. Jack reviewed his long-term memory. *He remembered a Harold Hartley*. He had been honored by the Templeton Society some twenty years ago. Gary had Googled his name and found that he had written a book entitled, *Without the Lord*, which gave a very negative view of what civilization would be like without religion.

The guys hadn't thought much of the book and passed it off as trivial rhetoric. The poker buddies were all atheists, and they knew that they would never be honored by the Templeton Society for their views. The Templeton Society was a more religious group of men.

Gary dropped a glass in front of Jack. Taking a sip loosened Jack's tongue.

"He sort of disappeared, didn't he? Except for the Templeton celebration, I can't think of anything he's done in the last fifteen years. Sort of dropped off the face of the planet. Any bets on what he's doing now?"

"Taking over the world?" laughed Gary. "No bets. I Googled him. Not much came up since 1993 when he wrote a paper called, *Controlling the Populace*.

"Can you get a copy?" asked Jack.

"I've been searching for one. It should give us some clue as to what's going on. I wonder what he's planning?" said Gary.

"No idea."

Jack moved to the next page, and the man with the blond hair looked up at him. This was the guy Mark had seen picking up the reports at the post office. His name was Guenther Baskilin, born April 15, 1978. He was six-foot-one-inch tall with blond hair and blue eyes and weighed 175 pounds. Born in Hamburg, Germany, he was now a naturalized American citizen. The paper gave his address as 320 Sycamore Avenue, the same as Hartley's.

Gary added a page that described his last place of employment at the Parteihochschule Karl Marx in East Germany until it closed in 1990. Jack wondered what Hartley and this handsome blond man would have in common.

"Did you Google this guy, Guenther Baskilin?" Jack asked holding up Guenther's page.

"A ghost. I looked him up at that East German university. It seems he died five years ago in a fire. I checked the pictures and other specifics and it's him. So what's a dead guy doing with the FSC?"

Jack turned to the last sheet. It was a green Jaguar owned by Ian Hartley, Harold's younger brother. Ian was also a political scientist and worked part-time at Boston College as a lecturer. The page held nothing more of interest. Jack put the pages back in the envelope and glanced up at Gary.

"What do these guys have in common?" asked Gary.

"Maybe our friend Harold wants to take over the world?"

SUNDAY

Harold Hartley slowly sipped his expensive Crown Royal whiskey straight up from a short, stout crystal glass. He relaxed in an enormous, black leather chair that had belonged to his father. His perfectly organized study included a large wooden desk and walls of bookcases filled with leather volumes. A large fire roared in the stone fireplace.

His younger brother, Ian Hartley, rested across from him. Ian preferred rye with ice as his poison. Harold thought his brother a simpleton for drinking rye over whiskey. The nature of Ian's alcoholic beverage choice had formed the basis of one of their petty arguments over the years.

Harold broke the silence, "Did you give the new list to Flo?"

"Of course," replied Ian, trying to avoid any anger seeping into his tone.

Ian gave Flo that list at the end of every day. It was part of Ian's routine, a routine Harold established for him. Harold planned everything for everyone under his command and thus maintained complete dominance.

It was generally acknowledged by their parents and friends that Harold had the greater intellect so Ian constantly felt inferior to him. And Harold had been very controlling ever since he was a child.

The sibling abuse had begun at an early age. Harold had forced Ian to do all his chores and had hit him until he complied. He also emotionally abused his younger brother by constantly telling him that he was stupid and not worthy to breathe his air.

Yet, Ian was drawn to his elder brother and always felt the need to follow Harold at everything. Both confirmed bachelors, they existed together as they always had in their family's ancestral home, except for a few years in their thirties when Ian had taught and lived in Holland while Harold completed a sabbatical in Germany.

It was well documented that both brothers were religious men opposing Darwinism and evolutionists. They wrote many articles about their strong and steadfast belief in God and the necessity of following the words of the Bible.

The luxurious room returned to silence. This was the only place in the house without surveillance cameras. It was also the only room no one entered except by invitation.

Harold required at least one place where his words would be safe from uninvited ears. He had microphones and cameras installed all over the house so that he could watch everyone at all times. He trusted no one and treated everyone like lambs on their way to slaughter.

A heavy, loud knock at the wooden study door shocked Ian into alertness. Harold waited while Ian rose from his chair and opened the door. They both knew it was Guenther. Guenther wouldn't enter the study until Harold gave his consent.

Guenther's main goal in life was to please Harold. He considered him a god. He would do anything for that man, even die. Ian envied Harold's ability to rule over everyone. People followed him without question. No one had the nerve or desire to contradict him. Whatever Harold said was law, which was the only way this dangerous game of theirs could be played.

"Enter," said Harold as Ian held the door open.

Guenther reverently entered Harold's study carrying a large red cardboard folder. Dressed in a black, long-sleeved shirt and black pants, Guenther stood stiffly in front of Harold. He bowed his head then handed over the thick red folder. Harold opened it and reviewed the green pieces of paper describing the delinquents. These were the Americans who either didn't return their reports in time or not at all.

With precision, Harold removed a blue fountain pen from his inside pocket of his dark blue suit jacket. Beside each name on the green sheet of paper, Harold wrote a number from one to five.

Each number designated the type of action to be taken against that person. A three required their files to be pulled and reviewed more frequently. Five was the kill order. There were very few fives, but a few more fours on the long list. A four meant they were to be watched. Guenther distributed the list to the appropriate co-workers employed specifically for the five or four assignment.

"Give this to Franz," Harold said to Guenther holding out the closed red folder.

Retrieving the papers, Guenther bowed his head then smartly turned around and left the room without speaking a word.

Harold had met Franz through Guenther, his cousin from Schwerin in northern Germany. He was the mercenary, the hit man – pure evil. He received his instructions and behaved accordingly without blinking an eye. For Harold's takeover to be complete, he needed men like Franz and Guenther.

As the heavy study door closed, Ian counted the number of occasions he had heard Guenther speak. There were few. When he did speak, brevity was the key.

Years earlier, Guenther had met Harold at a political science convention in Germany where Harold had been invited as a guest speaker. Guenther had been introduced to Harold at a seminar entitled, *The Changing Zeitgeist*, where Harold spoke about writing his own commandments.

Guenther began to spend much of his time with Harold who was delighted to install his religious beliefs into a young, intelligent disciple. Guenther was a willing sieve who left his family and his job as a teacher of political science to live with Harold in the United States.

Harold's large study was the control center, a private place to discuss his plans with Ian. But Harold had slowly and completely taken over and rarely discussed things with Ian anymore.

The brothers remained in Harold's study for another half an hour drinking. They discussed the importance of religion and how all Americans must follow the same faith. Then Harold wished Ian goodnight, Ian's cue to leave.

As the door closed behind Ian, Harold considered how he had concocted the present conspiracy. He had toiled for many years in the planning and organizing of this radical idea. From childhood, Harold believed he was destined for greatness. He considered himself the new world savior.

The reports proved the first step: getting everyone to spy on each other, was successful. But now, he thought about his next plan to take over the United States. Everyone would soon follow him and accept his new religion.

TUESDAY

Mark's cell phone rang. It jiggled on the bedside table.

"Hello," Mark said groggily into the phone.

"Mark? Mark? Is that you?" A frightened woman's voice spoke frantically into his ear.

Mark leaned up on one arm. With the other hand he turned on the lamp. His alarm clock read 2:10 a.m. Who the hell was calling him at this hour?

"Yeah, this is Mark," he growled into the receiver. "Who is this?"

"It's Maggie. Maggie from Starbucks in D.C."

"Oh yes, Maggie. Hi. What's the matter?"

"I got that package today from the FSC. I'm supposed to spy on a clerk in the hardware store across the street. What do I do?"

Mark sat up in bed now fully awake.

"Okay Maggie. Don't worry. Just write something boring about that guy and mail it in those white envelopes once a week. Write whatever you want. Just don't make it interesting. You'll be fine."

"But the letter said, if I miss a report, my life will be in danger."

"It won't be. I promise you." It was an empty promise, but it seemed to calm Maggie down.

Then Maggie remembered the other reason she called. She had been watching the post office every day and knew when the beeper went off. She identified the attractive blond man as the culprit. She always stood near the window waiting for him to come out of the post office. She would watch him jump into his silver SUV.

Mark was now sure that they had their man. Maggie didn't need to continue watching him.

"You can stop now. We've got enough information. Just hold onto that stuff and we'll get it from you soon."

He thought Maggie would fall apart but now she sounded relaxed and was even gently flirting with him.

"When are you coming back?" she asked.

Mark laughed softly into the receiver.

"I don't know, hun. Maybe soon. My friend Jack will be in D.C. tomorrow. Do you want him to stop by?"

"Sure. I can give him the journal and the beeper. Boy that directive sure scares the shit out of you, doesn't it?"

Mark agreed.

"Wish you were here," Maggie whispered.

"I wish I was too."

"What would you do if you were here?"

"Do you prefer nibbling or licking?"

"Licking."

Both Maggie and Mark sighed deeply into their receivers. Mark remembered that he had an early meeting and needed to sleep. He placated Maggie with a few more sexy comments before wishing her a good night.

She was worth a visit. Mark smiled. Then he put his head on his pillow and fell fast asleep. When he awoke in the morning, he was thinking of Maggie. The call was like a dream, and he wondered for a second if it had really happened.

WEDNESDAY

Out of the corner of his stern blue eyes, Guenther saw the yellow taxicab drive slowly pass him then park twenty feet away from the Hartley driveway entrance. It was obvious that the cabbie was spying on him, but he didn't know on whose behalf.

He wouldn't put it past Harold to check up on him. He just wondered why he had picked this idiot. He obviously wasn't playing with a full deck.

Guenther followed Harold back to the U.S.A. when Harold's sabbatical year ended and moved into his home. Harold met Guenther's every financial need as well as becoming a surrogate father to him.

Though he had a bright intellect, Guenther rather enjoyed his present subservience. He responded to Harold's every command with the quick efficiency of a military man and was fully prepared to obey Harold's plan to reduce the population of the U.S. to the status of religious slaves. Guenther was only marking his time. His ability to shine would appear soon. He didn't want to make a mistake and lose the power he hoped to command. He was prepared to follow Harold as long as necessary to reach his personal goal to rule the world.

The thick iron gates automatically swung wide open as Guenther drove his silver SUV up the curved, well-manicured driveway to the tall front doors of the historic mansion. The rounded driveway looked like a giant "C" made out of finely granulated white stone.

Opening the SUV's trunk, Guenther removed a large, black valise. Two guards stood at quiet attention while Guenther walked past them into the house. Everyone knew that to displease Guenther was to displease Harold. No one wanted the repercussions they heard could happen if they angered those men.

Guenther nodded to the long-serving butler who returned the gesture then left to attend to his other duties. Guenther walked across the grand foyer, which boasted a high ceiling. What looked like a large bulls-eye was inscribed in tile on the expansive floor. Guenther entered a deep, narrow room on the right where thirty people sat at computers entering information from the numerous spy reports extricated from the white, plain envelopes.

Guenther dropped the black case on top of a long, oak table lined with different colored trays. A young, blond-haired, brown-eyed man, who declared himself thirty-four but looked much younger, stood by the wooden table. He greeted Guenther with a stoic nod.

Many years ago, Harold had attended a private meeting organized by a group of young and influential people who believed in creationism. Andreas was one of the members and took an instant liking to Harold who stood up after some persuasion to divulge his personal thoughts on the subject. Andreas cornered Harold after the meeting, and the two struck up a friendship.

Guenther knew Andreas didn't like him because they were in a constant battle for Harold's attention. He didn't trust Andreas even though he was theoretically third in command. Andreas did what he was told, no questions asked.

With a consistency born of habit, Andreas grabbed the black case, opened it, and pulled out hundreds of white envelopes. He then sorted and laid the envelopes into the different colored trays. He couldn't wait until Harold caught up with the times and required people to email their reports.

The rainbow of trays represented the various numbered positions of Americans. Each of Harold's data entry employees was positioned in a double row at the large-screened, high-tech computers where they entered a constant stream of information.

These clerks had been hired from a special, private agency. Each one had been willing to give up family and friends for a period of time that was determined by Harold. They all lived in the east wing of the Hartley mansion. Four people shared a room, giving the wing a dormitory-like feel. When they signed Harold's contract of secrecy, each was paid a large sum of money. Another large sum would be paid to them when they completed their contract.

As their superior, Andreas walked up and down the windowless room while they worked. He watched them as carefully as if they were polishing diamonds.

Though everyone was terrified of Harold, they felt an intense desire to please him. He sometimes wandered amongst them saying how much he depended upon them. He was going to change the world.

WEDNESDAY

At the intersection of Wisconsin and Twinbrook streets, in Bethesda, Tony planted his taxicab in front of a Mom and Pop convenience store. Jack was sitting in the back. Both men were looking north along Wisconsin. The Walgreens delivery truck would arrive from that direction at any moment.

All the way from the airport, Jack listened as Tony explained the delivery truck's route. This small store was the last stop before 320 Sycamore Avenue, the truck's final delivery. Tony had drawn a thorough map showing the exact direction back to the Walgreens parking lot. Jack was delighted by Tony's penchant for detail. He was also pleased that Tony didn't ask any questions.

Ted and Mark were right, thought Jack, *grease this guy's palm and he's yours for life.*

Suddenly, both Jack and Tony bolted upright. The Walgreens truck had just stopped at the intersection before making its turn into the convenience store's parking lot. Jack jumped out of the cab, handing Tony a few one hundred dollar bills and a big thanks. He ran to the right side of the street.

The truck pulled into the parking lot to make its delivery. The driver parked the truck then jumped out with a metal clipboard in his hand. He went around to the back of the truck and opened the wide rear doors then hopped inside. While the driver was pulling out the items to be delivered, Jack retrieved the syringe from his knapsack. He flipped his bag on his back and inched closer to the parking lot and the truck.

The Walgreens delivery man emerged from the back of the truck with his eyes on his clipboard. He was dressed in starched, plain blue jeans and the required Walgreens long-sleeved, blue shirt. His brown hair needed a comb, and he could do with a new pair of shoes, but there was nothing remarkable about him.

Jack watched the delivery man take a trolley from the back of the truck and begin to load some boxes. The Walgreens driver checked his clipboard again then dropped it onto the top box and wheeled the load into the back of the store. The owner waited for him at the threshold of the screened door and held it open.

While the men were inside the store, Jack snuck up to the cab of the delivery truck and jumped in. There wasn't much room in the passenger side because of all the empty coffee cups, newspapers, clipboards, and other assorted garbage. Jack did his best to hide then put a black ski mask over his face.

Holding the syringe in front of him like a sword, Jack waited. He smiled at himself, feeling like Dexter Morgan.

He heard the empty trolley roll alongside of the truck. The delivery man put it in the back, then closed and locked the back doors. The front door of the cab swung open, and the delivery man hopped in.

Without taking a breath, Jack leaned forward and poked the driver's neck with the syringe. The delivery man jolted in shock then slumped over the steering wheel unconscious. Jack couldn't believe how fast Peter's drug worked.

Once sure that no one had noticed anything, Jack dragged the limp body into the passenger side. Before pushing him under the seat, he grabbed his car keys from his pocket. He checked the clipboards. Once he had found the one marked 320 Sycamore, he turned on the truck's ignition and drove to the Hartley mansion.

Thanks to the many pictures taken by Ted and Mark, Jack recognized the ornate, metal gate and high, thick, green hedges. Jack turned into the driveway and up to the gate. He sat there for a moment until the gates swung open as if by magic. Jack looked at himself in the rear view mirror and mouthed the words: *shut up and deal*.

After driving a few feet into the Hartley compound, Jack noticed numerous guards patrolling the periphery of the grounds. A sea of grass containing an occasional elm tree stretched out between the huge, silent mansion and the tall hedges that surrounded the property.

He could extrapolate from the serious and dedicated manner of the plain-clothes guards that they were concealing weapons. There was an air of arrogance and self-assurance about the men. Jack's eyes wandered over the park. With his right hand, he carefully held up a small video camera to record everything.

His blue eyes followed the road. He inhaled audibly. A mansion the size of two football fields came into view. It looked like a 17th century British castle. There were minarets at each corner. He had an eerie feeling and wondered if there were more guards standing in those towers looking out at him. What was he was getting involved in?

Jack slowly followed the stone lane that curved around to the back of the mansion. At the back door, two old men in black uniforms and aprons waited for him. The younger of the two came forward and a look of shock and annoyance crossed his face.

"Where's Scott?" he asked.

"Sick. Got stuck with his route today," answered Jack.

"Can I see some identification?" asked the older chef.

Jack handed over the fake identity card that Gary had prepared on Photoshop and hoped it would pass the test.

The men examined it then frowned.

"Fine, but see you don't forget anything," said the older chef with authority though Jack noticed a degree of fear and concern as well.

Copying the delivery man's movements, Jack reviewed the clipboard. He played with the keys looking for the one which opened the back of the truck. Luckily he found it quickly. He opened the doors then checked which boxes were to be delivered. This was the last stop so he gathered all of the boxes left were meant for this house. He loaded up the trolley and walked into the castle through the kitchen. His video camera was still hooked onto his belt. It looked like a cell phone and recorded everything.

Once inside the mansion, Jack handed the boxes to the kitchen staff who stored the goods in their appropriate places. While the chefs were busy elsewhere in the back of the kitchen, Jack walked as silently as possible across the huge, immaculate kitchen to a swinging door.

He opened the door, praying it wouldn't squeak. The next room was a spacious dining room with two long, black wooden tables. Each could seat over thirty people.

He leapt to the closest door on his right and poked his head through. He saw that it led to a long vestibule which he entered, giving the camera the opportunity to copy the scene. A large and intricate, glass chandelier hung from the high ceiling within a room filled with ornate paintings on every wall. Jack guessed the floor to be white marble. He could see a few rooms, but all they revealed were shadows on walls. Fearful of being caught, Jack ran back to the kitchen.

Grabbing the metal trolley, Jack saluted the chefs and took off out the back door. He threw the trolley into the back of the truck and locked it. When he jumped into the cab, he noticed that the real delivery driver was still out cold. Peter had said he would probably have an hour until the drug wore off.

Using the detailed directions Tony had provided, Jack followed the route back to Walgreens. He parked the delivery truck in the main parking lot alongside the other similar delivery trucks. He picked up the delivery man and positioned him at the wheel of his truck to make it look like he'd suddenly fallen asleep.

After sticking the keys into the ignition, Jack glanced around. No one could be seen. He slipped out of the passenger's side and ran out of the parking lot toward the taxi he saw down the street.

Tony pulled up alongside him and said, "Thought you'd need a quick getaway. Jump in."

Jack said a silent prayer of relief and slid into the taxi's backseat. He realized that Tony was bursting with questions since he kept turning his head to stare at him. It felt good to finally be safe, so Jack didn't mind talking. And he felt he owed Tony more since he had come to his rescue.

"So what's the place like?" asked Tony.

"Pretty big. British architecture looking totally out of place here in America. Obviously lots of people are working in there though I only saw the kitchen staff and the guards wandering around the property."

"Lucky you got out of there alive! Are you guys crazy or what?" Tony said into the rear view mirror.

"Crazy, no. Insane, yes," said Jack.

The two men burst out laughing.

As soon as Jack could breathe, he said, "Someone has to find out what's going on in there, so it might as well be us."

"Why don't you just go to the cops?" Tony asked.

"We don't know if we can trust the police, and we don't want the people at 320 Sycamore knowing about our spying. Yes, eventually we will have to get the law involved and take our chances, but which branch?"

Tony and Jack relaxed in silence, each in their own thoughts.

Finally Tony said, "Hey, where am I taking you?"

"The Starbucks at the corner of G and Pennsylvania. Can you wait for me? I'll only be about ten minutes." Jack had to meet this Maggie.

They arrived at their destination before too long. As Jack strolled through the front doors, he recognized Maggie immediately from Mark's detailed description. *Definitely Mark's type.* Maggie was flirting with a couple of male customers while preparing their coffee requests. He slid up behind them and waited his turn.

"I promise you, Maggie, my wife will never know," said one of the men.

"No, but I'll know," said Maggie. "Get out of here, John. Brad, take him away!"

The two regular customers continued to laugh, then grabbed their coffees. They left the café with a wave to Maggie. Jack smiled at their flirtatious conversation as he walked up to the front counter. He ordered his coffee and watched Maggie prepare his drink.

When she returned, he introduced himself bringing forth a beautiful, wide smile. She asked him to sit at the table in the corner, where she would join him in a second.

"Here's your journal and beeper," said Maggie as she sat down.

Jack picked them up and put them in his briefcase. "Thanks so much for your help, Maggie. We really appreciate it."

Maggie smiled then said, "Glad to help."

"Mark mentioned that you've received a package."

She nodded.

"Don't worry about it. As long as you keep sending in those reports, you`ll be ignored."

"Now I know why everyone is so jumpy. My nerves are fried."

Jack agreed. "I know what you mean. Just hold fast and we`ll be in touch."

Jack and Maggie rose from the table. Jack came around to her side and gave her a friendly hug.

Tony and his taxi still waited outside. Jack opened the backdoor and slipped inside.

"Back to the airport."

After a few minutes of silence, Tony said, "Do you still need me to go by the place?"

Jack thought for a moment then said, "No, I don't think so. You should stop in case you were noticed. We`ll contact you if you are needed again."

"Sure thing, pal. Glad to help."

At the airport, Jack handed Tony more cash and repeated his thanks for everything he had done for him today. Tony just smiled while patting the money in his shirt pocket.

Jack turned his back on D.C. with good riddance. He napped on the plane and was thrilled to see Ted at the airport to whom he shared his day's adventure. The poker buddies were making headway into uncovering what Hartley was up to but they were also putting themselves in grave danger.

THURSDAY

Instead of playing cards, notepads sat in front of everyone's chair at the poker table. Jack spoke first.

He took the better part of an hour explaining the abduction of the delivery man and his visit into the Hartley mansion. He handed out a large number of photographs taken with his cell phone. He had printed them out that morning. They all took turns memorizing them as if there would be a test later.

Next, Gary described the information he had discovered on the five vehicles shown on the surveillance tapes. He brought detailed sheets, which he was glad to get out of his house.

"So we've got an imminent creationist taking over the U.S.A. along with a dead guy picking up the mail," said Mark.

"How do we stop them? Do we go to the police or the newspaper?" asked Ted.

"Paper," said Gary. "I've got connections. I'll sound them out, and whoever is clean gets the story."

"We should call the FBI," said Peter. "These people are armed to the teeth. I'm sure they wouldn't hesitate to kill a reporter, but maybe they'd think twice if it was a cop."

"Good point," said Mark.

"Listen, we know what we'll be getting with a reporter especially one who has not succumbed to the FSC. First, we'll talk to him then we can call the cops," said Gary.

They all sat back in their chairs mulling over Gary's proposal. After glancing at each other, everyone agreed. They would allow Gary to find a journalist with whom they could discuss their findings and possibly obtain a way to inform the American public.

However, Peter could not sit still. The other guys noticed him wiggle in his seat and begged him to reveal what was bothering him.

"It's Laura. I think she's in danger," Peter said as he recalled his wife's drawn face.

"Why do you think that?" said Mark, sipping his beer.

"She discovered her spy and approached him."

"Who's her spy?" asked Jack as he passed out the cigars.

"Phil, an accountant, whose office is close to our pharmacy."

"What do you mean she approached him?" asked Ted, accepting a cigar.

"She caught him taking pictures of her while she was picking up Colleen and Chris from school. She was furious."

"I don't blame her," said Jack, lighting his cigar.

"Phil stood behind a tree on a neighbor's lawn. Laura strode over to him and confronted him."

"Wow," said Mark, putting down his beer. "That takes guts. What happened?"

"He became very angry that he'd been caught, but I think he was more scared than angry. He swore Laura would suffer."

Jack grimaced. "That's horrible."

"She's pretty sure he'll report those facts to the FSC," said Peter, shaking his head.

"Don't worry," said Mark after lighting his cigar. "We'll get to them before they can get to Laura. I'm pretty sure we can protect her."

"But if they get to Laura, they might learn about us," said Gary whose face scrunched up in worry.

"Good point," said Jack. He took a puff from his cigar and blew the smoke slowly into the air.

They all worried about what they were involving themselves in. Could they protect Peter and Laura and their two children? What if they were attacked or their families' safety became in jeopardy?

Instead of backing off, the poker buddies became even more determined to rid themselves of the FSC if not for themselves but for every American family.

THURSDAY, a week later

The card table wasn't set up, and the poker chips remained locked in the cabinet. Instead whiskey glasses, a bottle of Crown Royal, and Dominican cigars sat on the coffee table in Mark's spacious living room.

Gary had phoned and said he was bringing Michael McAlister, a reporter with the *Boston Herald*. Gary hadn't said much other than that McAlister, even though he had received a package, still wanted to bust the story open. He was willing to take a chance. McAlister was an old-fashioned journalist, always searching for the next big story that might earn him a Pulitzer.

Mark had heard of McAlister. He seemed to be a decent enough guy. His newspaper articles were always printed in the front news section dealing with political and scientific discoveries. McAlister had told Gary that he wanted the biggest story of the century: exposing the FSC and saving the United States.

Arriving first, Jack and Ted entered Mark's house. Mark told them about the guest while they commented on the empty poker table. Nervous about exposing themselves, the men sat together in the living room and talked about mundane topics.

A few minutes later, Gary arrived and showed McAlister into Mark's house. The men introduced themselves and shook hands. It was then that Mark offered a glass of whiskey to each man. They agreed to wait for Peter before discussing anything.

As the last to arrive, Peter burst through the front door and said, "I located a rare interview Ian Hartley gave during his college days. He mentions an elder brother who was also a scientist. He describes . . . Oh, I'm sorry," he said suddenly noticing McAlister. "Hi there. I'm Peter Node. I guess you must be the newspaper guy." Peter held out his right hand.

McAlister got up and shook Peter's offered hand. "Yes, I am."

"We think the FSC is being run by two brothers who are creationists and religious fanatics," said Gary who sat at one end of the black leather couch.

Ted sat next to him, while Peter took the black leather chair offered to him by Mark who was sitting in a black leather recliner. McAlister took the principle position in an ornately designed wooden chair with a padded seat and a carved design on its back. No one ever sat in that chair.

"You've all received packages?" McAlister began as he placed his small, black microphone on the coffee table.

He watched their faces as they all nodded in the affirmative.

"Okay. Then I don't mind revealing that I did too. I'm supposed to spy on this neighbor in my apartment building, but that guy's already scared shitless. If you made a loud fart, he'd hit the ceiling. I duly send in my weekly reports in those white envelopes, but it's all complete bullshit. I can't understand why he doesn't accept emails."

"Yeah, he's a bit behind the times," said Gary. "There doesn't seem to be a problem as long as we regularly send in those reports. I don't think it matters what we write."

McAlister smiled then asked, "What does the FSC do with all these reports?"

"They download the information into computers," said Jack since he had been the one who had seen the large computer room in the Hartley mansion.

"That still doesn't answer the question: what do they do with the information?" McAlister pushed.

Ted answered for the group, "We don't know. But have you looked outside lately? People are afraid of their shadows. The FSC has taken control of the country."

"Have you got proof?"

Pulling out a clear photograph of Guenther, Mark said, "This guy picks up the envelopes from the post office in D.C. I placed a wire device on the post office box." He then described Maggie's continual surveillance.

"Where does he take them?" asked McAlister, leaning forward. He picked up his pen and notepad.

"I followed him to 320 Sycamore Avenue in Bethesda," said Mark, sipping his whiskey.

After he had written down the address, McAlister asked "And who lives there?"

"Harold Hartley," said Jack, lighting a cigar.

"Who is he and what does he have to do with the FSC?" asked McAlister, holding his pen in the air.

"He's the conspirator," said Ted, leaning forward.

Thinking a moment, McAlister said, "Have you got proof?"

Gary sat back, crossed his legs, then said, "No proof now, but we will in time."

McAlister nodded his head as his microphone recorded every word.

Mark glanced at the machine then at McAlister and said, "These words you hear tonight could mean our death."

"Don't worry. After I transcribe the tape, I'll delete it. I'll keep the transcript in my safe. No one but me has access."

Noticing his friends' worried faces, Gary said, "I take full responsibility for bringing McAlister."

"We trust your judgment," said Ted.

Then McAlister said, "In the package, I read that a catastrophe would befall me if I didn't comply. Are any of you guys having any problems?"

"No, but there are often rumors of people suddenly disappearing," said Peter after butting out his cigar. He reached for the whiskey.

Jack sat up and agreed that he had heard the same thing at the high school where he and Ted worked.

"What else have you got?" asked McAlister.

"We've got pictures from inside the Hartley mansion. Something big is going on there," said Peter, sipping his whiskey.

"How do you know that?" asked McAlister turning to a fresh page.

Jack handed over his phone to McAlister who flipped through the photographs while Jack described the large kitchen, long dining table, and computer room with rows of computers.

"Looks like room for a lot of people," McAlister said. "But what are they all doing?"

"That we don't know," said Mark. "But you'd need that many people to upload all those reports."

"So, this Hartley is in charge?" said McAlister checking his recorder.

"Probably. Here's a copy of a few of his papers and books. Thought you might like to read them," said Ted, turning to his side. He picked up the material on the coffee table then handed them over.

"Can you give me a summation?" asked McAlister, trying to balance all of the papers in his hand.

The guys looked at each other but it was Jack who responded, "He writes like his opinion is the only one. A fanatically devout man, he believes religion is the only path to salvation."

Gary took over, "He's an arrogant, self-absorbed prick."

After everyone laughed, McAlister said, "I'll do some research on him and let you know what I find out. But I can tell you one thing, the FSC is dangerous and people are dying. Are you sure you're safe?"

"Good question," said Peter as he glanced nervously at the poker buddies.

Turning off his recorder, McAlister asked, "So what's your next move?"

"I don't know about you guys," said Ted. "But I think it's time we all disappeared. It's getting just too dangerous to hang around and then it would be easier to choose our next plan of action."

"We should get our wives and children out of here especially after what happened to Laura. Remember the cottage?" asked Jack.

No one voiced the location because of McAlister's presence, but they all nodded.

"Let's go there and now!" Jack continued. "Get everyone together there and we'll figure out what to do next."

Immediately, the five men stubbed out their cigars and downed the whiskey left in their glasses. They gathered their belongings.

"We'll keep in touch," said Gary to McAlister."

Everyone knew this was a big story and that McAlister would love to be the savior of the American people.

McAlister gathered the papers then rose from the chair. He walked towards the front door where Gary waited for him. Mark showed off one of his famous smiles usually reserved for women and shook McAlister's hand. Gary followed placing his hands on McAlister's shoulders and pointing him towards the car. Mark and Gary exchanged glances as if to say, *Drop the guy off and get home fast.*

As soon as his friends' cars had left his road, Mark glanced around the area, then closed and locked his front door. He ran over in his mind what he would need to take to Jack's cottage. There wasn't much. Then he remembered Maggie. Before packing his laptop, he sent her an email advising that he would be in touch soon.

FRIDAY

Ted, Susan, and their two boys, Justin and Andy, reached Jack's cottage first. The family dropped their luggage at the front door and immediately searched the place for any video recording or listening devices. They checked behind every lamp, picture, bookcase, electric socket, and vent. Not until they were completely sure the house was bug free did Susan speak.

"Is anyone hungry?"

Her family burst out laughing.

"Rhetorical, mom," smirked Justin.

"Okay. Why don't you find our rooms and make the beds? I'll get the kitchen going," said Susan, gathering the bags of food.

"I'll join you in a sec, mom," said Andy. "We'd better make tons since the others will be starving when they arrive."

Susan carried the groceries into the kitchen and got to work. Ted and the boys collected the rest of their belongings and carried them upstairs to the bedrooms they usually inhabited when they visited Jack and his family.

Everyone called Jack's place in Nantucket a cottage, though it was more like a city mansion than a lake cottage. The property had been originally bought by Jack's grandfather though it was his father who built the present house. Jack's father had made a lot of money in the stock market and spent much of his later years here.

The cottage consisted of seven fully equipped bedrooms and five full bathrooms. The rooms had been simply decorated with paintings and art work given to them over the years. The basement contained a large, old-fashioned, green-felt pool table, a fifty-two-inch television, an assortment of workout equipment, and the washer and dryer.

The main floor encompassed a well-organized kitchen and a dining room with a table large enough to seat an entire basketball team. The main living room boasted a great stone fireplace surrounded by brown-striped couches. Two smaller bedrooms flanked the far side of the main floor. A magnificent stone chimney ran through the house with vents on every floor to keep the cottage heated.

Busy in the kitchen, Susan broke three dozen eggs into a large metal bowl. With a whisk, she beat the eggs adding salt, pepper, onions, and cheese. As she was browning sausages and bacon on the stove, Andy arrived. Ted and Susan were sure that Andy would make an excellent chef one day. He loved being in the kitchen. Susan watched as Andy expertly cut up the potatoes and roasted them in a big baking pan.

"Mom?" Andy asked, as he sautéed the vegetables. "This ruse of a stomach illness isn't going to work for long. Sooner or later someone from the high school is going to call you."

"Don't worry. No one knows we're here," said Susan as she emptied the bowl over a heated pan covered in butter.

"How long will we have to stay here?" Andy asked while he turned over the sausages and bacon.

"Who knows? Who knows how long this thing will take to play out?" Susan scrambled the eggs.

Andy hesitated then said, "Do you really think Dad and the guys have the answer?"

"Yes. I hope so. We have to remain positive and optimistic. Can you watch the eggs while I get out the bread?"

"Sure, mom."

Suddenly, car doors slammed shut outside. Susan and Andy ran out of the side door and Ted and Justin burst out the front one. The men helped Jack with the suitcases, and Ruth fell into Susan's arms. They both heaved a huge sigh of relief.

Jack turned to Ted and asked, "Have you heard from Gary?"

"No, but I spoke with Mark. He was packing up and said he'd be here sometime tonight." Ted picked up a few suitcases and tucked them under his arms.

"Peter called me just before we left. They're right behind us," said Jack, grabbing the other bags. "We're going to have to make some definite plans as soon as possible. When was the last time you filed a report?"

"Yesterday." With long strides, Ted followed Jack into the house.

"I mailed mine today. We've got at least two weeks before they begin to look for us." Jack backed into the door and held it open.

"Do you know who your spy is?" asked Ted lugging the suitcases over the threshold.

Following Ted up the stairs, Jack said, "Yes, he's a math teacher at Nelson."

Ted stopped moving, stared at Jack then said, "Mine is John Beasley."

"John? Our neighbour?" Jack asked as he stretched his back. "Are you sure?"

Avoiding the children rushing all over the house, Ted and Jack climbed the stairs and strode into the main bedroom. After dropping the luggage at the foot of the bed, Ted closed the door.

"Yes, I'm sure," Ted finally replied. "It was like he forgot he was spying and would just stand on his lawn staring at our house. When I talked to him, he wouldn't look me in the eye."

"Did he see you leave?" asked Jack, dropping onto the bed.

Ted reviewed his departure, "Possibly."

He had glanced at the Beasley home while packing the car. Their car was gone from their driveway, so Ted assumed John was out when they left.

Opening the bedroom door, Jack said, "I corralled a few necessities yesterday. Come help me get them out of the car."

By the time Ted and Jack had removed the rest of his luggage from his SUV, Peter, Laura, and their two children, Colleen and Chris, arrived. Knowing the kids would be playing by the beach, Chris ran towards that end of the property. Colleen joined the adults in the kitchen to look for Renee, Gary's daughter, who was her best friend.

The sound of an arriving car alerted the residents, and all the men moved to the front of the cottage in time to see Gary arrive with his wife, Anne, and their daughter, Renee. Gary parked the car and the men helped with their luggage. Anne and Renee joined the other women in the kitchen.

When the scrambled eggs, bacon, sausages, toast, and hash browns were ready to serve, the children loaded their plates then walked downstairs to the basement. There they played video games and watched television as they ate. Their parents huddled in the kitchen. The mood was somber because the road ahead seemed long and dark.

Each of them had seen the faces of their co-workers, friends, neighbors, and even strangers. The whole populace seemed to be on edge, nervous, and stressed out, an atmosphere of strained panic.

"No one looks anyone in the eye anymore," said Peter thinking about the last few weeks at his pharmacy. "They'd just stare past you as if you're talking to a ghost."

"Everyone seems terrified to say too much because they did not know who was watching or listening," said Gary, munching on a piece of toast smeared with strawberry jam.

"I'm glad we got away from that," said Ruth, heaving a sigh of relief.

Suddenly, Peter's cell phone rang. Everyone's eyes turned towards Peter who realized it was Mark when the caller's number was displayed on the phone.

"Hey Mark," Peter said as much to Mark as to the rest of the group.

"What? . . . Yup . . . Okay . . . See you soon."

After he hung up the phone, Peter explained, "Mark's being followed. He's taking the long route to lose his shadow."

In their minds, they reviewed their drive. Everyone felt a chill down their spines, fearing that they too had been followed. Jack and Ted looked at each other, took big steps to the windows, and gazed out into the mid-morning light. Gary opened the front door and walked into the forest. His eyes darted in every direction. He checked each car ensuring they were locked.

Peter went out the back door and checked the view for any signs of movement. He then walked around to the front of the cottage and met Gary. Together they turned around to the others and made the "Okay" sign with their fingers.

Back in the kitchen, Jack said, "I'm sure we're all safe," confirming what they felt.

"C'mon everyone," said Ruth. "Eat!"

Accepting the command, everyone picked up their plates and finished eating in silence. But soon that silence was interrupted by a herd of children returning their plates to the kitchen or seeking seconds.

Once they were alone again, Gary said, "So, as McAlister said, what's our next move?"

"You said Ian Hartley leaves the compound twice a week in his Jaguar," Jack said to Ted who still watched the hidden cameras he had placed in the hedges of the Hartley mansion.

"Yes why? What's mulling around in that head of yours?" said Ted as he spooned some eggs into his mouth.

"What if we kidnap him?" asked Jack, pushing his finished plate into the center of the kitchen counter.

Everyone dropped their cutlery and looked at him.

"Kidnap him?" asked Ruth looking like she had seen a ghost.

"We could get Tony to follow him and find the best place to pick him up," said Peter.

Susan began to shake. "His disappearance will cause an uproar at the FSC."

"We don't have to kidnap him for long. Just long enough to determine what's really going on," said Jack, playing with his fork.

"Why pick Ian?" asked Ted concerned about where this was leading.

"He's not smart enough to concoct this whole FSC thing. You've read his books and papers. Not one original thought," said Jack.

When he finished chewing a piece of bacon, Peter asked, "Where do we take him?"

"What about Maggie's place?" Gary suggested.

The women blanched and said in unison, "That would put her in danger."

Gary jumped in, "We'll blindfold him and tie him up. He won't ever see our faces or ever see where he is being held. I think we'll get more out of him if he can't see anything."

"Okay," said Jack. "I'll call Tony and put him on Ian's trail. See what he digs up."

He pulled out his cell phone and flipped through his address book until he located Tony's name. After pleasantries had been exchanged, Jack said, "Could you follow Ian Hartley's green Jaguar?"

"Sure," Tony said. "Be glad to."

"Take notes of everywhere Ian travels and what he does," said Jack.

"No problem. Oh, by the way," said Tony. "I got one of those packages you mentioned. Have to spy on some lawyer on my route. I occasionally drive him home. I'm following the instructions to the letter but not writing anything interesting. Don't worry about me. I'm with you guys."

"Glad to hear it, Tony," said Jack gesturing to the others in the kitchen that Tony had been enlisted by the FSC.

"Keep that frame of mind," Jack said. "Call me anytime. My friends and families are holed up in a special place. We're safe. Thanks for all your help. Bye for now."

Now everyone they knew had been compromised by the FSC. Harold had complete control, but what was he going to do with all this power?

TUESDAY

With the excited feeling of embarking on an epic adventure, the five poker buddies piled inside the red Toyota Sienna minivan they had rented at the airport. They drove from the airport to Bethesda using the detailed directions given to them by Tony. Jack maneuvered the van through the city streets until they reached their destination: the Vintages parking lot. The wealthier elements of society favored Vintages, a specialized liquor store.

Although Ian Hartley frequented many different stores, he was always in public view. However, when entering the liquor store, he parked in the store's back lot, which was reserved for those customers who did not wish to be seen. Here, Ian was alone and the poker buddies would be able to capture him easily.

The red minivan slowly edged its way into Vintages' back parking lot and settled down to wait for Ian. In nervous silence, the five men focussed on the driveway.

About twenty minutes later, a green Jaguar pulled into an empty spot in the middle of the parking lot. There were no other cars except the red minivan, which was parked at the far end.

The men watched Ian slink out of his car and rush into the liquor store like a mouse being chased by a cat. Jack started the minivan, pulled out, and parked beside the driver's side of the Jaguar. The men then drew black ski masks over their heads. Gary and Ted crouched beside the sliding door of the van. Peter had a blindfold in his hands and Mark sat in the front seat next to Jack.

They didn't have to wait long. After a few minutes, Ian dashed out of the liquor store and made a beeline for his car. He seemed a little nervous about the minivan parked so close beside him.

Gary opened the door just a crack. When Ian stood beside his car about to open the front door, Ted pulled the minivan's door wide open. Gary took Ian's right arm, and Ted grabbed his left. They lifted him and his recently purchased liquor into the van. As soon as he was inside, Peter put a blindfold around the man's eyes then patted him down looking for a weapon but none was found. Once Gary grabbed the liquor, Ted tied Ian's hands behind his back.

It all happened so fast that Ian didn't even have a moment to react. When he finally caught his breath, Ian shouted, "Do you know who I am? Do you know who you're dealing with? You're dead men. Dead men."

"Calm down, Mr. Hartley," said Mark. "We're not going to kill you. We just want to talk to you."

"Talk, ha. So you know who I am. Then you know you're all dead men," Ian said squirming in his seat.

He spoke with greater bravado than he felt. He was obviously frightened.

"You don't scare us," said Gary with a laugh. "We know you and your brother are playing some sort of dangerous game."

"It's no game. It's the greatest experiment ever achieved. My brother is brilliant," shouted Ian.

"So, what's your plan?" said Mark.

Ian Hartley laughed while he tried to wiggle out of the arm restraints, but Ted's knots were tight.

"Who are you guys?" Ian said as he tried to look at them from underneath the blindfold but there was no chance of sight.

"No one of interest," said Gary as he buckled Ian into the seat beside him.

As soon as everyone was settled, they took off their masks and Jack started up the motor. He pulled out of the Vintages lot, leaving Ian's Jaguar behind.

"Where are you taking me?" Ian said in a quivering voice.

"No place you'd know," said Ted who sat beside him.

Jack slipped into the light traffic on Goldsboro Road. From Connecticut Avenue, they proceeded to Tilden Street NW. As they neared their planned destination, Jack turned into a quiet neighborhood with pleasant rows of dark orange townhouses.

It was a nice middle class area with an immaculately clean street and manicured lawns. The townhouses were probably fifty or sixty years old judging from the extent of the foliage on their lawns.

Jack drove to the end where Maggie's house waited. The guys were impressed with the area and wondered how a Barista could afford such a nice place.

Maggie had parked her blue Hyundai Accent on the street to leave the driveway open for Jack. Mark was pleased that Maggie had agreed to allow the poker buddies to use her home. He knew she'd agree to anything in order to see him again.

When Jack turned the engine off, Peter handed Gary another blindfold, which he tied around Ian's mouth. Jack and Mark exited the minivan first and carefully looked around to see if anyone was about but the neighborhood was silent except for an oncoming vehicle.

As soon as the car passed them, Jack said, "Now!"

Gary and Ted guided Ian out of the van, along the white stone pathway, and up the front steps to Maggie's townhouse. Maggie held the front door open. She appeared nervous yet sexy in tight black jeans and a low cut pale green blouse that showed off her eyes. Mark put his fingers to his lips and blew her a kiss. She smiled but, as they'd agreed on the phone, said nothing.

The men half-carried, half-dragged Ian into the house. Maggie pointed to the left, which led into a spacious, pleasant living room area. All the lights were on since the curtains were drawn.

The men deposited Ian on a comfortable flower patterned couch that was part of a five-piece living room set. Ted sat on Ian's right on the couch, and Jack took the other side. Gary sat on the recliner and immediately pulled the lever so his legs had somewhere to rest. He leaned back and stretched out. Mark sat beside Peter on the loveseat.

Jack leaned over to Ian and pulled off the material around his mouth. Ian stuck out his tongue and wet his lips.

"Is the prisoner allowed a glass of water?" whispered Ian.

As if by command, Maggie entered carrying a pitcher of iced tea and six glasses. She filled one then handed it to Jack who had his arm outstretched. He held it to Ian's lips.

"You're dead men!" Ian spat out as soon as he took a breath of air.

"You'll never be able to identify us, Mr. Hartley. We won't keep you for long, only as long as it takes you to tell us what's going on," said Gary.

Ian adjusted himself on the comfortable couch then sat in silence. The guys followed suit. They all noticed his lower lip quiver.

"Come now, Mr. Hartley," Jack said in his best consoling tone that he often used with delinquent children. "What's your brother up to?"

"You'd never understand," Ian said.

"Try us," said Ted, leaning towards Ian.

"Only men of true intellect like my brother and I can understand." Ian twisted his hands, but he couldn't wiggle out of his bonds.

"What do you do with those reports you collect every week?" Peter tried a different tact.

Ian was taken aback. His mouth hung open and his body tensed. But Ian, instead of being smart, puffed out his chest and spoke haughtily.

"It's ingenious really," said Ian with a bold laugh. "We've succeeded in tracking every adult in the United States."

The men spoke to each other with their eyes. Gary asked, "For what reason?"

With arrogant pride, Ian said, "We're creating the perfect society."

"Utopia doesn't exist," said Mark, sitting back on the couch.

"We'll create one."

"With everyone afraid of their shadow?" asked Jack, crossing his legs.

"That will end soon" Ian tried to look under his blindfold.

"How?" asked Gary. The men exchanged a shocked expression.

"Everyone will soon receive a new package. In it will be instructions about following our new religion."

Jack's mouth dropped. "New religion? Do go on."

"The American people need a real god. Someone they can follow and who will actually answer their prayers."

The men laughed. They wondered when God would enter the picture.

"And who is this god?" asked Mark.

"Harold Hartley," Ian said with obvious pride.

"Yeah, right," Gary said rocking in his chair.

Ian closed his eyes under the blindfold and spoke slowly, "We're giving Americans what they need. They're drowning. My brother will save them. They'll learn the importance of believing in Harold and what Harold can do for them. He is the new God."

"Do you really expect Americans to do your bidding?" said Ted, leaning forward.

"They do now, don't they?"

"We'll stop you!" Mark replied.

The others nodded furiously definitely agreeing with him. They had a good read on their opponent.

"Tight group huh?" Ian said feeling the connection. "We'll break you. We've got a few specialists who'll do what's necessary to retain power and control. You'll conform or die."

"Not likely," Jack snorted.

Ian shrugged his shoulders and said, "Then you'll die."

Mark called his bluff and said, "You'll have to find us first."

"We'll find you. You can't hide from us," spat Ian.

Ian pursed his lips. He wouldn't provide any more information. It was obvious that he had said enough already, but he didn't seem to be the type of man who knew how to keep his mouth shut.

Realizing this, the guys smiled at each other while Peter returned the cloth to Ian's mouth. Nodding to each other, Gary and Ted grabbed the disagreeable man and put him into the back seat of the red minivan.

When goodbyes had been said to Maggie and with a quick kiss from Mark, they all piled into the vehicle and returned Ian to his Jaguar in the Vintages parking lot. The guys wondered if he would tell his brother about his kidnapping and if there would be any repercussions.

WEDNESDAY

Rolling over, Mark enjoyed watching Maggie's trim body rise from the bed and head towards the shower. He would join her in a second, but he needed to review his thoughts.

She was quite a woman. She had handled herself better than he had hoped, and now she had proved herself to be a capable lover, a little kinky, but he liked that. She was definitely not a one-nighter. Mark mulled over the idea of inviting her to Jack's cottage.

Rising, he moved over to the window and looked out into the neighborhood. It certainly looked peaceful. Birds chirped and leaves waved in the gentle wind.

A few townhouses away, a man left his home. Mark watched him look up and down the street while walking to his car parked on the street. As he put his key into the car lock, he looked over the top of his black Pontiac then quickly jumped in.

Mark watched as the vehicle drove out of the neighborhood. He wondered if it was a coincidence that another car parked a block away also left as if following the Pontiac. The street returned to peacefulness.

The shower water slipped off Maggie's body. Mark stared at her through the thin, clear shower curtain. He smiled with what he imagined awaited him and stepped into the bathtub.

* * *

No one was surprised to see Maggie in Mark's Mercedes Sport when it pulled up to Jack's cottage. The men had told their wives how helpful she had been and about her obvious interest in Mark. They both appeared refreshed and relaxed. The group smiled at each other.

"Let me help you with that," said Jack as he picked up her suitcase. Mark grabbed his bag and a briefcase.

When Maggie reached the front door, Ruth introduced herself. She then introduced her to the other wives and the few children lurking about curious about the newcomer.

Joining Mark and Maggie, Jack pointed them upstairs where he showed them into the last bedroom. The rest of the group flowed into the kitchen to make lunch.

They had a good assembly line going. Ted and Jack buttered the sandwich bread while Peter and Gary added slices of luncheon meat and tomatoes. Ruth and Anne made French fries, and Susan and Laura made a huge batch of potato salad. The kids set the dining room table and two folding tables that had been set up for them.

It was a large, noisy meal with much laughter. It seemed as if these people didn't have a care in the world. Maggie was initially a little frightened to be thrown into this big mix of obviously very familiar people. She had liked the men who had come to D.C. so she was sure she would like their wives.

Everyone was being very kind to her and she was glad to be away from the city. Since less people were coming into Starbucks, there was little need for two Baristas so her boss approved her vacation without comment. She was so much happier here. Her eyes caught Mark's gaze. He winked at her.

After the dishes were washed and put away, the kids ran outside to play, while the adults adjourned to the living room. They had recorded Ian's interview so that they could review his words. The men needed to hear it again and they wanted their wives' input.

Every time Ian brought up God, there was a noticeable sign of uneasiness from the group. The women turned to their husbands whenever Ian threatened them with death, but they trusted their men and respected their decisions.

"We must stop them," said Gary, standing up.

Everyone nodded in agreement, but no one spoke. Each person was lost in thought, trying to come up with a strategy to stop the Hartley brothers.

SUNDAY

In the evenings, the Hartley brothers could be found relaxing in Harold's study sipping their preferred alcoholic drink. Harold rarely initiated conversation unless it was an order or command, and Ian never opened his mouth unless his elder brother spoke first.

Tonight, Ian wondered how to face his brother. He had hidden his abduction. The kidnappers had returned him to his car along with Harold's whiskey. It was as if his disappearance had never happened.

Even though Ian insisted upon doing his own errands, he consistently disobeyed Harold's command that he never leave the house without a bodyguard. But a bodyguard would only be in the way. He had assured Harold that he was safe only to be proved wrong. From now on, he would use a bodyguard.

But talking with those men had made Ian ponder his situation. What place would he have in Harold's new society? Harold's Commandments were only revealed to him after they had been sent out to the populace. What was his brother hiding from him?

Guenther acted as more of a confidante to Harold than he was. Ian was jealous of Harold's attention to Guenther even though he knew Harold saw Guenther as the son he never had. Ian glanced at his brother who seemed content in his chair with a smirk hanging on his full lips.

Precisely at eight-thirty, one loud knock on the heavy wooden door shattered the silence. Ian looked over at his brother, knowing he would never move to answer the door. Ian rose and invited Guenther to enter. Guenther immediately scurried over to Harold, bowed then handed him a red file folder.

"Your copy of the Commandments and directive, sir," said Guenther. "Your subjects will receive it tomorrow."

Smiling broadly at Guenther, Harold accepted the offered file, which he slid down beside his body. "Good work, Guenther. Now email your friends and have them ready. They'll be required if we find dissension."

"They're all prepared."

Ian had heard that Guenther had organized a group of men in every major city in America to follow his command. These men had been handpicked by Guenther but Ian didn't know where he had found them.

"Good. No mercy. The people must learn obedience," growled Harold glaring at his brother.

"Is that really necessary?" Ian said, squirming uncomfortably in his chair.

The assemblage of misfits Guenther had corralled would not hesitate to commit physical torture or hand out severe punishments. Ian believed that only Harold could make the world a better place, but he was concerned about Harold's method. When Ian had read the Commandments, he had been shocked at the vehemence of some of them. If Americans didn't obey Harold then violence would ensue.

Guenther answered for Harold, "Very necessary."

Guenther would commit any act for his mentor and now god. Ian knew Guenther had little regard for him and thought he was inferior. Ian also knew that Guenther wanted nothing more than to prove Harold was their savior.

"My dear brother, it's a necessary route and we must investigate all means. Why don't you work with Flo this week and help her review the reports?"

Flo had told him that she needed someone to take over reviewing the reports so she could keep up with the census of each town, city, and state. It was a tiresome job, but Flo never complained. Ian knew she was truly dedicated to Harold and a little in love with him. They had met many years ago when Harold lectured at the university she had attended. She had followed him ever since.

The job Harold offered his brother was a tedious and time-consuming deed. Flo would also be his boss, and he would have to report to her. Ian would not show his displeasure in front of Guenther. This was his chance to show his brother that he was capable of any job in his empire.

"I'm happy to do whatever you wish, brother."

Harold then completely forgot about Ian's presence and conversed with Guenther about the next step in their campaign. Harold rose from his comfortable chair and maneuvered his way to his enormous, walnut desk.

Unlocking the middle drawer, he handed Guenther a note handwritten on a piece of green paper. "Email this to everyone tomorrow. Then mail the package. One for every household."

"I swear it will be done."

Guenther carefully slid the paper into a notebook he carried at all times. Harold might say something of importance and he would have to record it. He hung on Harold's every word.

Harold sat up straight in his chair and said, "I want no dissension. If you notice anyone not accepting my rules, then their life must be terminated. One dissatisfied fool leads to others. The people must follow me."

Standing up, Guenther said, "The people will follow you. You're God."

"They'll follow me after tomorrow. I'll guide them to a more fulfilling life, and they'll realize how much better life will be with me to lead them." Pushing back his chair, Harold rose while Guenther stood at attention.

"I beg to learn from you."

"You've succeeded well, my son," he said placing a hand on Guenther's head. "You're a true believer. Once your men are in place, I'll be sending you on some errands." Harold smiled at the word *errands*.

Still resting by the fireplace, Ian listened to Harold and Guenther's conversation. He worried about that word. He knew what it meant. He wished Harold could complete this takeover without violence, but Guenther was a violent man and was looking forward to that part of the mission.

Guenther laughed. "We're ready."

"Good. We'll speak more tomorrow."

Harold closed the drawers of his ornate desk left to him by his father. The desk, known as the "Monster," had been in his family for many generations and had always been used by the head of the family. The many intricate carvings and drawers were made out of smooth maple wood. A few of the iron rings on the desk led to hidden chambers, but they were only known by the owner of the Monster.

No one but Harold sat at this desk. There was no reason for anyone else to be near it with the exception of the housekeeper who cleaned the Monster every day. Only she was allowed to touch the desk, and she applied many hours to polishing that wood.

Realizing that Harold had dismissed him, Guenther bowed. With quick, long strides, Guenther glided across the length of the study and was out the door before Ian realized he was now alone again with his brother.

Tentatively, Ian glanced over at Harold and realized that Harold wanted him gone as well. Quickly saying goodnight, he took his leave and made the journey up the stairs to his bedroom in the west wing. There was so much Ian wanted to say to Harold, but Harold hated his questions. For the time being, he followed Harold because Harold was God. He would wait until the time was right.

MONDAY

On this day, every adult in the United States received an email, which included a list of directives. In addition, every household received a small green paperback book entitled, *Harold's Prayers*.

The printed paragraph stated:

> *Congratulations, you have been accepted into the new world and a better way of life. Read, memorize, and review your new Commandments. You are to follow these Commandments. Failure to comply will end in retribution. Do not discuss these matters with anyone. That is against the law. It is now your duty to live the good life. If someone challenges this good life, they must be reported. I shall lead you to paradise.*

The other item in the email was a document entitled *Harold's Commandments* listing fourteen rules:

1. Harold is now your only God;
2. Harold's Commandments must be followed under threat of personal disaster;
3. The Bible must be followed under threat of personal disaster;

4. We are descended from Adam and Eve. Any other belief will be met with personal disaster;
5. Your new faith is Haroldism. Everyone, no matter what religion or background, automatically becomes one of Harold's followers;
6. Every individual over the age of thirteen must pick a house of worship and must attend said place of worship every day;
7. Each person should keep their copy of *Harold's Prayers* at hand, enabling you to study it at every opportunity. Being found without your copy of *Harold's Prayers* could prove disastrous;
8. Each house of worship will receive the new prayer book. Non-compliance will result in destruction of your communal building;
9. We are now one people. Anyone who deviates from this pattern is our enemy and must be reported;
10. Every life is important and, therefore, anyone causing death to another human will be executed immediately. There will be no abortions or genetic manipulations. Anyone involved in such behavior will be executed immediately;
11. To possess wealth is no longer your goal. Money is no longer important. Harold will teach and guide you;
12. Every person over the age of sixteen must complete at least one hour of community service every day. You will find a list of charities in *Harold's Prayers*. Everyone must volunteer with at least one

charity. Non-compliance could be personally disastrous;

13. Anyone caught committing a crime as charged by the Law Courts of the United States will be put to death immediately. By ridding ourselves of this lower class of individuals, we will better our society. Jury trials will no longer be necessary. Harold's Judges will make the final decision;

14. You are now free. Cast off your coats of unhappiness. Harold will lead you to a happy, healthy life. The chance for miracle bonuses in life is now a reality.

MONDAY

Tony emailed the poker buddies Harold's note and the fourteen Commandments, following up on Mark's request that he forward along anything he received from Harold Hartley.

After dinner, the poker buddies and their wives congregated in the living room to discuss Tony's email and attached document. Jack read aloud the rules. The further down the list they went, the more they wondered why anyone would follow such idiocy. Every aspect of their lives was being controlled by an insane man.

"We have to stop him!" said Gary, jumping to his feet.

"Nobody's going to follow this. It's ridiculous," said Anne, reaching out to her husband to calm him down.

"I don't know," said Mark. "While driving here, I noticed how slowly the traffic was moving. I didn't see anyone weaving in and out of traffic. You rarely see an accident now."

"Well isn't that one good thing?" said Ruth, sitting on the edge of her chair.

Everyone tried to smile.

The mood was somber, yet everyone's wheels turned in their heads. Once in a while, someone would look up, shake their head then lower their eyes.

Everyone wondered what it would take to defeat Harold Hartley.

The group couldn't believe that people would blindly follow him. Unfortunately, most Americans were a rather conservative and religious lot who tended to follow blindly. This group of atheists wondered how they would be able to reach them over Harold especially if he threatened personal disaster.

"We have to get in there," said Jack. He sat back in his chair and crossed his legs

"Get in where?" said Susan shocked out of her silent revelry.

"Into the Hartley manor. We have to learn how to defeat him," replied Jack.

"That's too dangerous," said Ted, bolting upright in his chair.

"Yeah, maybe but what choice do we have? We have to decide the best course to stop Hartley," said Jack, throwing up his hands in the air in the form of a question.

He stared at his friends daring each one to think of a better plan. They all shook their heads. There was not much else they could do.

"I'll do it," said Mark as the only single man in the group.

Jack bowed his head then looked up, "No, thanks Mark. It has to be a woman."

"A woman? Why?" cried Ruth.

"Remember? A vehicle with three women was noticed entering the Hartley mansion. We should find out more about those women and then replace one," said Jack.

Peter went pale. "Won't she be discovered?"

"Let's find out about these women first. Perhaps it isn't the same women every time, and one of our wives can infiltrate them," said Ted, rubbing his hands. He understood where this was headed.

"Okay, we'll start there. I'll call Tony in D.C. and ask him to follow that vehicle and find out what he can," said Mark. "It should be relatively safe."

"Right," said Peter, though the rest silently thought about what Jack had proposed.

Mark rose from the leather sofa and gently patted Maggie on the knee. She smiled lovingly at him showing her resolve to assist in whatever way she could. However, she hoped she would not be picked to infiltrate the Hartley mansion.

Mark called Tony and explained what the group proposed. He asked Tony to figure out the identity of the women. Tony recognized Mark's description of the black Hyundai Accent from his days spying on the mansion.

"Of course," said Tony. "I want this craziness to stop."

Then, it occurred to Tony to ask, "Have you contacted the police?"

"No, we're not concerned about that right now. We need more evidence," Mark replied.

"Well, if you ever decide to go to the law, I know of a police detective. He's a pain in the neck, but he's an honest guy. He always follows us taxi drivers, expecting something devilish to occur. I could sound him out if you'd like?"

"Hold on a sec," said Mark.

"Sure pal. Your dime," said Tony.

Putting down the cell phone, Mark said, "Hey guys, Tony has a connection with the police. Should he contact the guy?"

Everyone blanched and looked around the room. They had been afraid to go to the police in case the tables turned and instead of putting Harold behind bars, they would be in danger.

"Are the police siding with Harold?" asked Gary. shrugging his shoulders.

"We don't know," said Jack. "Maybe Tony should check out this cop."

Retrieving the phone, Mark said, "Sure. Talk to your cop friend. Try and find out how far Harold's power goes."

"His name is Constable Mike Verns or 'The Taxi Detective' as we prefer to call him. I can't wait to find out what he knows and what the police are doing about it."

"Neither can I."

"He's pretty involved with the police department and, if there was anything to find out, Constable Mike would know."

"But how much will he be willing divulge, if anything at all?" asked Mark.

TUESDAY MORNING

Tony sat nervously at a small table in his favorite coffee shop. He crossed then uncrossed his legs. His hands shook. Adjusting his uncomfortable tie, he awaited Constable Mike. He was both eager and frightened to ask the questions burning in his mind.

Glancing constantly at his wristwatch, Tony wondered when he would arrive. He had cornered the Constable yesterday after he saw him following another taxicab. Tony pulled his taxi behind Constable Mike's police vehicle and flashed his high beams. Eventually, Constable Mike pulled over and got out of the police cruiser to find out what Tony wanted.

Out of the corner of his eye, Tony noticed Constable Mike enter the coffee shop. He was smartly dressed in his police uniform. Mike removed his cap and placed it under his left arm, and then he waited in line to give his order to the pretty young woman behind the counter: a black coffee with a chocolate donut. He carried his breakfast to the two-seat, wooden table where Tony sat waiting.

The two men had been sparring partners over the years. Tony didn't like Mike, and Mike didn't like Tony. Tony and the other taxi drivers disliked the constant police attention and awaited Mike's appearance with a feeling of dread.

142

As he sat down at the table, Mike snarled, "Good morning. What do you want?"

"Good. Right down to business," said Tony putting down his coffee cup. "I'm not quite sure how to approach this topic with you. It could be dangerous."

Constable Mike leaned in narrowing his eyes. "I won't repeat this conversation with anyone, but you better not be playing me."

"I'm not, but I have to ask you something first," said Tony. He clenched his shaking hands.

"Shoot."

"Are you involved with the FSC?"

"I wondered if you would be asking that," said Mike changing his tone. "Yes, I've received the same packages you've received and, yes, I had to spy on someone."

"How are the police handling it?" said Tony as he sipped his steaming hot coffee.

"No one at the department is willing to prosecute him. It's like everyone's in a trance."

"Everyone's blindly following this organization and following their mandates. Would you ever have imagined that everyone would attend a church again?"

"I know. It's unbelievable. What's going on in that mind of yours?"

"This has to remain between us, okay?"

Constable Mike nodded.

"I've been working with these guys from Boston who are trying to stop the FSC," said Tony. "Is there anything legally that we can do?"

"The law won't get involved at this stage. Everyone is too afraid of retribution. Some guys in our department have received threatening emails if they don't comply with the FSC's orders."

"Can you do anything?"

"Not at this moment. I have no one to back me up. But let me talk to some officers on the force. I'll get back to you. Okay, have to go. Early start today. We'll talk more tomorrow," said Mike, finishing off his donut and coffee.

"Thanks, Constable Mike."

"You have yourself a good day."

Mike downed the last drop of coffee from his cup and rose from the table.

Tony couldn't believe that even the police had no power over this Harold guy. He looked at his watch. It was eight-thirty-five a.m., about time to begin his shift. He wanted to finish early so he could follow Harold's women in the Hyundai Accent.

Tony dropped his coffee cup off on the main counter and left the café. His taxi was parked across the street. He couldn't believe how quiet it was even though numerous people walked the sidewalks and many cars were stuck in rush hour traffic.

Tony turned on the "Available" light and started the motor. He proceeded down the street driving fast enough to keep up with traffic but slow enough to be waylaid by a pedestrian searching for a ride. At the next corner, he noticed a couple standing by the side of the road. The man had his arm out. Tony slowed his vehicle and stopped right beside the couple.

These days, each person who entered his taxicab was a test case. Who was being controlled by the FSC? Who was rebelling? His passengers seemed to be complying with Harold's laws. He wanted to determine who was trustworthy and who was not by listening to how they conversed.

The couple who slipped into the back seat were immaculately dressed in suits of a dull shade. She wore a beige skirt, a plain white blouse, and a beige jacket. He wore a dark blue suit with a white shirt and a plain dark blue tie. Neither person was remarkable except for their conversation, which Tony eavesdropped on.

After the man had informed Tony of their destination, he turned to his companion and said, "Thank you for meeting me. You haven't returned my calls."

Tony watched them periodically through the rear view mirror which he slowly adjusted to allow him a better view.

"I didn't think it was safe," she said softly.

"Yes, yes I know. We have been careful, but you can trust me," replied the man.

"Can I?"

"Of course you can. We've been together two years now. You can always trust me. I promise you I won't let anything happen to you."

"How can you be so sure?"

Tony could see her body shaking as she covered her face with her hands.

"We will obey *Harold's Commandments* and do as we're told. I'm sure if we continue on that path, no one will notice us. Come on, cheer up. We'll go to my place, and I'll make you a delicious dinner followed by our favorite dessert. What do you say?"

The woman beamed. "Yes, Todd. Whatever you say."

Todd tried to move closer to put his arm around her but she shooed him off saying, "Not here."

Todd and his girlfriend sat almost touching in the back seat. They smiled at each other. No more words were necessary, and Tony saw from his rear view mirror that Todd had cheered up his girlfriend well enough to allow her to relax. After reaching their destination, Todd gave Tony a good tip which Tony appreciated.

After pulling away from the curb, Tony thought about the couple's conversation. They thought it was best to just follow Harold's rules, keep their heads down, and survive. They were willing to just continue their lives as quietly and as simply as possible. Their dress and demeanor showed that neither wanted to bring attention to themselves.

Throughout the rest of the day, Tony picked up a variety of people but mostly singles. No one was interested in talking, and his clients politely ended any discussion he tried to initiate. They would sit in the back seat and look blankly out of the side window.

At precisely six-fifty p.m., Tony waited one block away from the Hartley mansion at 320 Sycamore Avenue, Bethesda. He had a clear view of anyone leaving the ornate metal gates.

As expected, a black Hyundai Accent exited the Hartley driveway and turned left when reaching the street. Tony started up his taxi and followed. The black car drove onto the GW Parkway, and Tony diligently followed it a few car-lengths back. The Accent made its way into the city where it came alongside a tall office building.

Tony parked his car and watched the two women leave the backseat and enter the office building. Tony turned off the motor, jumped out of his taxicab, and followed them. He joined them in the elevator and noticed they pressed the button for the ninth floor. Tony exited the elevator on that floor as well and watched them enter an office.

When he reached the office door, he read the name: Harvey Girls Maid Services. He took out a piece of paper and wrote down the address, which he would forward on to the guys. He hoped this information would help them but wondered how dangerous it would be to get involved with this agency. They looked legit but he didn't know if they could be trusted.

TUESDAY AFTERNOON

While surfing the Internet, Gary noticed an email arrive from Tony. He read the information and smiled. They would have no problem filling the position of a house cleaner. Anne had worked in a hotel to supplement her income during her university years. Gary wasn't sure he wanted to volunteer his own wife and possibly put her in danger, but they had no choice. They had to see Harold's organization at close hand.

Printing out Tony's email, Gary made his way outside, where a volleyball game was in progress. The poker buddies played against their children. Even though this was a fairly innocuous sport, the men were very competitive. Their children were equally as intense as they attempted to beat their fathers. The women stood on the sidelines cheering each point.

Everyone stopped what they were doing when Gary walked to the court's sidelines. Gary held up Tony's email and explained his idea about a replacement maid. The group sighed. Now they had a plan to consider. But who were they going to send to replace one of the maids?

"Me," announced Anne.

Gary nodded solemnly and agreed with his wife that she was the best candidate to go undercover. He hoped she wouldn't be in any danger but was frightened to admit his feelings.

Renee ran into her mother arms. Anne did her best to reassure her.

After discussing the matter, the group located an inauspicious, quiet hotel close to the Harvey Girls Maid Services' downtown office. Gary would station himself there and wait for his wife to return every night. They would forward their progress on to the group.

Gary and Anne decided to leave for D.C. the next day. The sooner they got this over with, the better. Jack booked them a flight and printed out the plane tickets. Everyone spent the afternoon giving advice to Anne.

Interrupting the ongoing conversations, Jack said, "If you can figure out who's involved that would be great. Make note of everyone you see."

"But be careful," warned a worried Ruth. "Don't take any chances."

"I won't," said Anne.

"If you have a chance, get a look at this Harold. There aren't many pictures of him on file," said Mark.

"I'll try," said Anne.

Anne and Gary wandered over to Jack's study. Once settled behind Jack's modern glass table, she dialled the Harvey Girls' telephone number and received a happy receptionist who said, "Hello, Harvey Girls. May I help you?"

"Hello. My name is Anne Patterson. I've just moved to the D.C. area and I'm looking for work. I worked for three years with the Hilton hotels."

"Well, you've come to the right place. Can you come into the office at ten tomorrow? We're a little short at the moment and could use some new cleaners."

The receptionist gave Anne the office's location, which Anne pretended to write down.

Anne and Gary returned to the living room and advised everyone of their success. Jack offered to drive them to the airport. They expected to spend a week or two in D.C., enough time for Anne to learn everything she could. But they worried about the unknown danger.

* * *

Jack, Gary, and Anne drove in silence to the airport, their minds were flip-flopping through the enormity of what they were attempting. Gary was proud of his wife for taking on such a dangerous mission. All their friends were stunned by Anne's confidence and her seemingly relaxed attitude. Gary knew that Anne was the best woman for this job, but he was worried. He had no idea what Harold would do if Anne was discovered snooping while pretending to be a cleaning woman.

Waiting at the D.C. airport, Tony greeted them as they slipped into this taxi.

After Tony had comfortably settled into city traffic, Gary said, "So you're the famous taxi driver? Nice to meet you. I'm Gary Martin, and this is my wife, Anne."

"Nice to meet you. Are you *the* Gary Martin? Host of *Science Today*?"

"Yes, I am. Do you listen to my show?"

"Wow! I've got a celebrity in my cab. Yeah, that's one of my favorite radio shows. Every time I listen to you, I learn something," gushed Tony.

Gary and Anne laughed, glad to have something to lighten their mood and take their minds off their dangerous mission.

"Thanks, Tony. Glad to hear it," said Gary. "Do you have any news for us? Mark said something about you talking to a cop."

"Yeah. I know someone on the force. He's an asshole but a good cop. I spoke to him this morning, and he'll get back to me. I didn't tell him how involved you guys are."

"That's good," said Gary.

"I just said that I know people trying to discover any way to stop Harold. Was that all right?" said Tony, turning onto I-395 North then onto Route 1.

"Yes, sure," said Gary. "We'd be happy to relay our findings to the police."

"Okay, pal. I'll see what I can do. If you need any help while in D.C., give me a call."

"There is one thing," said Gary.

"Anything," said Tony.

Gary leaned on the front seat then said, "Could your cop friend obtain fake identification for Anne to back up her story?"

"I'm sure he could. I'll speak with Mike tomorrow."

Tony handed over his business card to Gary who said, "You're our eyes and ears, Tony. We rely on you for any information."

"You can count on me," said Tony, with an open sincerity that both Anne and Gary felt refreshing.

Taking the William Taft Bridge, Tony made a left turn at the third light onto Woodley Road. The entrance to the Washington Marriott Wardman Park hotel appeared on their left. Tony parked the taxi in front of the hotel and hopped out to retrieve Gary and Anne's luggage.

While shaking Tony's hand, Gary handed him two crisp fifty-dollar bills. All the guys had described Tony's love for money and he was obviously thrilled with the cash.

Tony gave Gary a big smile and said, "I'm meeting Constable Mike tomorrow morning. I'll relay what I learn."

"Thanks for your help, Tony. We really appreciate it. I'll be in touch," said Gary. He picked up their luggage and followed Anne into the hotel.

Walking straight through the massive, ornately decorated lobby to the front desk, Gary confirmed his hotel reservation with the pleasant-looking young man behind the main counter. Once the paperwork had been completed and they'd received their key, Gary and Anne took the elevator to their room on the eleventh floor.

Dropping their bags onto the floor, they threw themselves onto the bed and made love. It was sweet yet aggressive, something they hadn't felt with each other since they first married. This was the first time in a long time that they were alone. They enjoyed this sense of freedom but at what future cost?

THURSDAY

After a leisurely breakfast in the hotel's dining room, Anne made her way to the Metro subway and headed to the Harvey Girls office. Using Tony's instructions, she took the red line to 13th Street, then exited the subway and made her way into the sunlight. The office building was a short walk from the Metro.

Upon reaching her destination, Anne made her way over to the elevators and hit the button for the ninth floor. When she reached the floor, she followed the directions to the Harvey Girls office. Opening up the large glass doors, Anne entered the office and walked immediately over to the main desk.

"Take a seat in the waiting room. I'll contact the manager," said the pretty receptionist.

In due course, a well-dressed woman in a light brown suit arrived. She approached Anne and invited her into their conference room.

As soon as they were seated at the large, black conference table, Anne handed over her resume, which she and Gary had put together. She waited while her examiner reviewed it.

"Nice to meet you, Miss Patterson. My name is June Brooks. I'll be evaluating you to determine if you're the right material to join our organization."

Anne smiled widely and straightened her back hoping she appeared as a happy pleasant soul, perfect for any job.

June continued, "I see you've worked for three years at the Hilton. Good background. We have an opening at a retirement home. Are you capable of that?"

"Yes," smiled Anne. She was prepared to do or say anything to get hired. She wasn't surprised she wasn't given the opportunity of cleaning the Hartley mansion. She figured she would have to prove herself first.

June smiled back at Anne. "Have you worked in D.C. before? Your resume just lists New York references."

"I just moved here from New York. I've yet to find a good job."

"Do you have any specific hours you wish to work?"

"No, I'm capable of working any shift."

"No kids at home to worry about?"

"None."

"Excellent. I'll require a security check, but if everything is clear, then I could place you with this team."

Anne handed over Mike's concocted fake documents. She hoped they would pass the test.

"I'll email you the address and location of the retirement home if you pass our security check."

"Thank you, June. That sounds perfect for me. I'm looking for something regular and permanent."

"Good. I'll run the check this afternoon. Please call me by four p.m. I'll let you know then when your employment will commence."

With great relief, Anne rose from the stiff-backed office chair. Anne held out her hand to June, who shook it warmly. The women returned to the waiting room. Anne smiled and thanked June then left the office, pleased with her success.

With a light but driven step, Anne exited the office building and found herself back on 13th Street. After a quick look around, she located the Metro's entrance and again took the red line back to the Marriott hotel, where Gary waited for her.

* * *

Gary spent the entire day sounding out government officials. He had a few connections in the White House and was prepared to use them. With most calls, he was able to get through to someone's secretary; however, it was another thing to get past them to obtain an interview with their boss.

These officials worked in the higher levels of government and were nervous about a radio talk show host calling them. For months, Gary had been unsuccessful in scheduling interviews with anyone from the government. No one would even return his calls.

The poker buddies found it strange that the White House was so silent during the country's public turmoil.

The only thing Gary learned was that Harold had blackmailed the president and other high-ranking officials, which was the reason why they wouldn't do anything to stop Harold's plan for domination.

After making all of his initial phone calls, Gary spent a few hours crafting proper questions. He didn't want to scare anyone off, yet he wanted to learn the truth.

By early afternoon, a number of secretaries had returned his calls, all with sad regrets and excuses.

Undeterred, Gary explained, "I'm not taping this. This is a personal interview. I won't publish it."

After some pleasant banter and pleading, some of the secretaries agreed to refer his additional message on to their bosses. Gary had a lovely sounding, deep voice that usually attracted the ladies. His telephone manner was articulate and charming. He had made a good career choice.

No one at the radio station had questioned Gary's decision to get off the air for a while. It was becoming dangerous to speak publically, though Gary's show appeared innocent enough. It was a science show where most of the followers were atheists or at least non-religious. Gary was open with his atheism, and his listeners now wondered if he was in trouble with the FSC for that reason. Because of such concerns, the stationmaster agreed to Gary's request for a leave of absence.

After hours of phone calls and a lot of worry about Anne, Gary was about to explode when Anne opened the hotel door. He looked up from his busy papers and was happy to see her smiling face.

They fell into each other's arms, content with what they had accomplished that day. Both had so much news to tell the other, but they were very careful about what they said in the hotel room. They were sure it was bugged and anyone could be listening. Anne kept her news to herself until they were on the street.

The couple headed out to find a restaurant to consume a late lunch. Walking slowly arm in arm, Anne revealed how her interview went.

They located a small quaint restaurant with a lovely menu. Once inside and at their table, Gary revealed his morning's endeavors. He was still rather optimistic that one government official would return his call.

At precisely five minutes past four p.m., Anne called June Brooks at the Harvey Girls agency. June answered the ringing phone after a few moments. Her security check had gone through.

"Could you start tomorrow?" June asked.

"Yes, of course."

"Would you please come into the office after your day's work has been completed? We'll finish off the paper work then. I'll email you the directions. You'll join three other woman cleaning the retirement home."

"That's fine."

"Every day after work, would you please come into the office so we may approve your hours? You'll be paid every week on Friday. Does that meet with your approval?"

"Yes, thank you."

"Fine then. Welcome to the Harvey Girls. See you tomorrow," said June hanging up the phone.

Anne told Gary the good news. No calls came through to Gary, so the two returned to the hotel and fell into bed, succumbing to their love for each other but fearing what would happen tomorrow.

FRIDAY

After Tony arrived at the coffee house and retrieved his cup of coffee, he sat down at the table in front of Constable Mike with an air of expectation.

"Boy, have I got news for you," said Mike.

"What?" said Tony.

"I've spoken to a few police officers. This Harold guy must have some important friends in the department because no one's willing to build a case against him."

"Wow. That's not good."

"The guys are paranoid. The station is as silent as a cemetery."

"So we're on our own?"

"I'll conduct some discreet investigation. What about your Boston friends? Have they got any evidence against Harold or the FSC?"

"I've got their report for you here. It's quite a read."

Tony handed Mike a square, brown envelope that held a number of printed pages that he had received from Jack last night.

"I'm angry. I want to help those men stop Harold before it's too late," said Tony.

"I agree, but we won't receive much help from the police. There are a couple of guys I think I can trust. We're meeting tonight."

"Great. Let me know how it goes."

"Thanks and keep this quiet. Just between you and your Boston friends. If this gets out, we're dead men," warned Mike. "Okay, off to work I go."

Tony showed off his bright white teeth. Mike laughed, slapped Tony on the right shoulder, and marched out the coffee shop's front door. Tony remained a few more minutes. He wondered what else was going to happen today.

* * *

From the Harvey Girls' email, Anne printed out a map showing the exact location of the retirement home. She easily found her way since there was a subway stop very close to the home. She didn't have far to walk once leaving the subway.

The building looked like a retirement home with its severe lines and plain beige bricks. A few residents sat outside by the front doors. They were obviously enjoying the fresh air, but their faces were blank. Anne smiled at them as she passed.

She made her way through the front doors and into the reception area. She announced herself at the front desk. After handing over her fake documentation, the senior pointed to the back room where she would meet up with the other cleaners.

The chief Harvey Girls' representative gave Anne a list of the rooms she was responsible to clean. It was an easy and uneventful job. These elderly people generally kept their simple rooms clean and it was just a matter of vacuuming, dusting, and washing floors.

After Anne had completed her work, she waved goodbye to her co-workers and made her way to the Harvey Girls' office. There she handed in her hours then completed the final paperwork after handing over her fake driver's license and birth certificate.

Over the next week, Anne worked hard cleaning the elderly residents' rooms. She enjoyed the mindless activity. However, she had very little contact with the other cleaners. Her days were eventful. At the end of her shift, she dropped in to the Harvey Girls' office to hand in her hours.

One day, while in the office, she overheard a couple of women arguing.

"I won't clean that house," said one woman, standing near the receptionist's desk. "That place terrifies me."

"Neither will I. I bet it's haunted," the other woman said.

"You wouldn't make it out alive."

Anne made her way over to the women and asked, "What job are you talking about?"

"Cleaning that horrid Bethesda house," said one woman.

"Which house is that?" Anne asked, coming to stand beside the women.

"We don't know the owner, but the place is scary. No one wants to work there," the other woman said.

June, the manager, came up to the women and asked, "Have you made your decision?"

"Yes," said the first woman. "We won't take that job."

June turned to Anne and said, "What about you?"

"I'm up for a challenge," said Anne.

"Okay good," said June. "The hours are 9 a.m. until 7 p.m. You'll be working with two other Harvey Girls' cleaners. Ms. Barrett will collect you every morning in front of this office building at 8:30 a.m. She's been cleaning this home for approximately two years. They're very special clients, who require honest and trustworthy cleaners."

"When do you want me to start?" Anne asked.

"You might as well start on Monday. You can finish out your week with the retirement home."

"Sounds good to me."

Anne shook hands with June then headed out of the office. She couldn't believe her luck. She bet that house that no one wanted to clean was the Hartley mansion. She wouldn't be sure until Monday but it looked promising.

When Anne returned to the hotel, she told Gary the news. He was also optimistic and congratulated her on her success. They spent the weekend preparing and looking forward to Monday.

Monday

Anne reached the Harvey Girl's office just before eight-forty-five a.m. She was introduced to Debbie who guided her out of the office tower and out into the street. She stopped by the curb.

"Angela picks us up in here," said Debbie, looking out for Angela's car.

Anne took this opportunity to examine Debbie. The skinny young woman was probably in her early twenties. Though her soft brown eyes showed innocence, her blond hair was certainly dyed. She didn't appear very bright which is probably why she had agreed to take this cleaning job.

When Angela Barrett's black Hyundai Accent pulled up to the curb, Anne recognized it from Ted's photographs. Debbie entered the back right seat and Anne took her place in the left back seat.

Debbie introduced Angela to Anne as the new girl. Anne noticed that Angela critically examined her before starting up the car. Periodically, she stared and squinted into the rear view mirror. Though Debbie kept up a running commentary about her date last night, Angela said nothing. Anne took a distinctive dislike to Angela though she did her best to suppress it.

Angela's mousey brown hair was, like Debbie's, tied back into a simple ponytail. She also wore a Harvey

Girls' uniform though she had a dark blue jacket over her light blue starched dress. Her startling blue eyes were cold and fierce.

During the twenty-minute drive to Bethesda, Anne tried to appear as relaxed as possible, but butterflies jumped around in her stomach. She couldn't wait to see if she was actually going to the Hartley mansion, but she felt obligated to comment on Debbie's words since Angela remained silent.

"Have you been to that new Italian restaurant on Wisconsin Avenue? I think it's called Filomena something," said Debbie.

"No, I haven't," said Anne.

"It's so good. Expensive, but wow the food is amazing."

"That's nice."

"My boyfriend took me there last night."

"Oh lovely. Was it a special occasion?"

"I thought he was going to propose."

"Did he?"

"No. He just got a promotion at work and wanted to show off his new money."

By this time, Angela had turned into the Hartley driveway. Anne recognized it from the photographs, her heart pounded against her chest. She reminded herself to breathe and remain calm.

Angela stopped beside the gate's intercom system and pushed a button. Without a word from her, the ornate metal gate doors swung wide open.

Driving to the back of the mansion, Angela pointed the vehicle into a small parking lot and parked between Guenther's silver SUV and Harold's limousine. Grabbing her purse, Angela exited the car. Anne shadowed Debbie and jumped out of the back seat.

Angela walked into the mansion through the same back door Jack had entered. While pretending to keep her eyes on Angela, Anne was really looking at everything she passed. Mark had provided her with a little black video camera that looked like a harmless broach. It allowed her to record everything. Back at the hotel, Gary observed Anne's every movement.

The cleaning women strolled through the enormous kitchen and took a side door that led into a room that was filled with every kind of cleaning product ever invented. Anne was in awe of the number of bottles of bleach, floor cleaner, Clorox, Borax, and every shape and size of broom, mop, and vacuum.

Angela commanded her to take a mop and pail. Debbie did the same. She was instructed to remove a bottle of cleaning liquid from the shelf and pour it into the pail. Then she mixed it with hot water from the large sink in the corner.

Once their pails were full, Angela maneuvered the two women down a long passageway into the east wing of the Hartley mansion. There were numerous rooms off the east wing hallway. Anne took note then followed Debbie's example and began mopping the floors.

As they walked through the house, Anne noticed a number of surveillance cameras fastened to walls and ceiling. She worried about appearing on them so she kept her head lowered.

She was surprised that no one was around. The east wing was completely devoid of life yet every bed had been slept in. Who were these people? The neat rooms were painted an off-white colour, and the single wooden beds were topped with a light wooden headboard. It seemed to be Angela's job to dust the few pieces of furniture.

Once the east wing was thoroughly cleaned, the women returned to the maintenance room to rinse their mops, pails, and dust rags. Then they prepared to clean the west wing.

This side of the house was covered with solemn black, brown, and grey wall paper inscribed with hunting scenes. Huge paintings of different family members hung in the hallway revealing a long history rich in wealth and heritage. The subjects were all dressed in their finest silk or linen suits with shining jewels on their shirts and around their necks.

Only six large bedrooms opened off the west wing. The first two included sitting rooms filled with large, dark furniture as well as generously decorated bedrooms. The last four rooms were smaller but just as ornate. The rooms were immaculately neat and organized. Nothing was out of place. These splendid rooms were thoroughly cleaned.

Anne memorized everything. She looked for anything of consequence that would help her understand what Harold was all about. As quietly as possible, she opened drawers and closet doors looking for anything out of the ordinary, but nothing appeared. It was all just the usual stuff that any man would possess.

Next, the women returned to the main floor. When they had finished cleaning the kitchen and dining room, Angela turned to Anne and said, "We're going to clean the rest of the rooms on the main floor now. You're not to ask any questions or speak to anyone. Just do your job."

Anne nodded. She did her best to remain calm, but her body shook from fear.

While the women were back in the maintenance room, Anne could overhear a number of people moving into the dining room. When the area was clear, Angela led Debbie and Anne into the main vestibule, which had an enormously high ceiling with a beautiful and decorative stained glass round window in the center. Though it wasn't the sunniest of days, the sun's rays pushed through enough to bathe the extravagant area in a warm yellow light.

Once the vestibule was spotless, the three women moved into the adjoining rooms, which were all very neat and tidy. Anne couldn't find any dirt or mess anywhere, but she washed those floors to a mirror shine.

She was glad that she didn't run into anyone. Being her first time, she hoped to remain anonymous. She was terrified at being discovered.

Taking her aside, Angela pointed out a thick wooden door. "Never enter that room."

Anne was intrigued and pretended to stretch so that the camera would photograph the door. She hoped Angela didn't notice.

Then, Angela showed them into a long, narrow, white room. Along its middle lay a long white table filled with desktop computers. The computers were evenly spaced along the stark table with screens pointing in both directions so that many people could work at the table at one time.

Anne understood from Jack's pictures that she was now cleaning the room where everyone's personal information was being stored. She looked for an opportunity to examine one of the computers, but she was never alone. If only she could get just a few minutes . . . .

It was all seemingly well-choreographed the way the people who worked in the mansion and the cleaning women never bumped into each other. The maids were invisible to the people now eating in the dining room. She remembered a big, long table where probably thirty or more people sat. She also considered the number of bedrooms.

On the one hand, she was glad to remain anonymous, but she had to get a look at the people living here. Obviously, they managed to be kept hidden by only appearing when the cleaning women were somewhere else.

Once all the main rooms had been cleaned, Angela led the women back to the maintenance room where they cleaned their mops and pails. Anne could hear people moving from the dining room back into another room as their voices slowly disappeared.

Once everything had been put away in its proper spot, they walked out of the mansion through the back door. While passing through the enormous kitchen, Anne watched the chefs and their assistants clean up after dinner. Obviously they had just served a meal to many people proved by the many piled dishes and food all over the counters.

It was seven-twenty p.m. when the cleaning women returned to the downtown core. Debbie and Anne exited Angela's Hyundai Accent and made their way up to the Harvey Girls' agency to leave their hours.

Once in the office, Debbie said farewell and disappeared. Anne made her way back to the Metro. She couldn't wait to hear what Gary had to say about her day since he had watched the whole thing on his computer screen.

* * *

In the living room at Jack's cottage, the four poker buddies, their wives, and Maggie waited anxiously for Gary's evening call about Anne's progress. Everyone had applauded Anne for obtaining the cleaning job at the Hartley mansion. They had been worried she wouldn't get it when she was assigned to a retirement home. It was considered a small miracle that she had been given the position at the Hartley residence.

However, the group was terrified she had put herself at great risk. They had no idea how much danger Anne would be in if she was discovered as a spy.

When Jack's phone rang, everyone jumped out of their chairs even though they had been expecting the call. Jack answered after one ring.

"Gary? What's the news?" said Jack.

"Not much. Just a regular day cleaning the Hartley residence," said Gary.

"Regular day?" Jack laughed. "How could cleaning the Hartley place be normal? Did Anne notice anything?"

"No, nothing yet. But the place is covered in surveillance cameras and it seems that a lot of people are living there."

Gary described the many features of the Hartley mansion. He relayed explicit details concerning the long computer room and explained how he could build a special device to search the Hartley computers. Anne would set it up the next time she cleaned that room. Jack congratulated Gary on Anne's efforts, which he transmitted to the group when he hung up the phone.

"I hope Anne won't be discovered," said Ruth. "She could be in grave danger."

"Gary's watching her all the time," said Jack, tucking his phone into his jean pocket. "She'll be fine."

"Are you sure?" Laura said in a louder than usual tone.

"Nothing is for sure," said Mark in a solemn tone.

"If she's discovered, she could be killed," said Ted, rising to his feet.

"Are you sure?" asked Laura. Her body noticeably shook.

Peter put his arm around his wife's shoulders then said, "These people are dangerous."

They continued to worry about Anne. Was she in any danger? Would she be discovered? They looked at each other for answers, but found none.

TUESDAY

Waiting at the coffee shop's entrance, Constable Mike held two cups of hot black coffee. Tony was surprised to see him waiting there. After he took a cup of coffee, Mike nodded his head towards the street. The two men walked past a variety of stores opening up for the day's business.

"I don't want to talk in the café," said Mike, taking slow steps. "I'm worried about being overheard."

"Good thinking," said Tony matching strides.

"I've been working on this thing all weekend."

"What have you got for me?"

"It was extremely difficult digging up anything on this Harold guy. He hasn't done much publically in a long time. No criminal record, and his driving license is clean. But men calling themselves the Followers of Harold are involved in the disappearance of people all over the U.S. I can't prove it, but I have records of people disappearing or dying for no apparent reason."

"I've heard whispers, but I didn't know it was fact."

"It's a fact. I'm going to search the department's databases for commonalities between these disappearing people. I'll have something more for you by the end of the week."

Mike tossed his empty coffee cup into the nearest garbage bin. Then, he slipped his briefcase on top of the bin and took out a small brown envelope before quickly closing the case. He pretended to throw the papers into the garbage, but he magically passed them to Tony. Tony slipped the envelope under his jacket and into his pants.

"In there is a USB stick containing the victim reports and what I could find out about Harold in the police database. Pass them on to your Boston friends, but keep it quiet. If anyone knew I had copied those papers, we'd be up shit's creek without a paddle."

Tony chuckled at the vision. "No problem, Mike. No one will link you to these guys except for me, and I'm as quiet as a mouse."

Mike smiled and patted Tony on the back. "Got to get going. Lots of paperwork. Talk to you soon. Stay safe!"

"Thanks. I will," said Tony as they parted ways.

Tony turned and headed back to the coffee shop. He needed more caffeine. Once the coffee was safely in his car's cup holder, Tony drove around the downtown core searching for fares. He didn't have to wait long. As he approached the next block, he spied a young man looking for a taxi.

* * *

While the Harvey Girls scrubbed the vestibule floors, Guenther rushed past them towards the long, white room across the hall. He carried a heavy leather valise. Anne pretended to stretch, thereby allowing the tiny camera to get a good shot of the blond man. He was the first person she had seen while cleaning the Hartley mansion.

Anne worked her way around the vestibule so that she was close to the computer room door and had a good view as Guenther slipped inside. The rows of computers were each being utilized by people who sat directly in front of a screen. They were so intent on their work that no one noticed Guenther's brief presence.

When Guenther exited the computer room, he almost tripped over Anne's pail, which was placed in the center of the hall. Cursing under his breath, he glared at Anne.

With a sweet, subservient smile, Anne quickly retrieved the spilled pail, bowed her head, and prayed that Guenther would leave her alone. She kept her head lowered. She didn't want to bring attention to herself especially from this man. Though her hands shook, she continued to wash the floor.

Guenther raised his fist as if to strike Anne but instead stormed off. Breathing a huge sigh of relief, Anne worked hard to leave the large vestibule sparkling.

While the women were in the maintenance room, all the people from the computer room moved towards the dining room to have their evening meal. Anne could hear them talking though she couldn't make out their words.

Once the air was silent, Anne's team was directed into the long computer room. While Angela dusted the computers and the various tables situated around the room, Debbie and Anne set their sights on the floor, which seemed just as spotless as the rest of the mansion. Anne found it amazing that their services were required so often since the mansion appeared perfectly clean.

Moving about the room, Anne searched for the perfect time to install the USB stick her husband had programmed. She watched Angela and Debbie carefully waiting for any moment when their attention would be diverted.

Angela completed her work first and waited for Debbie and Anne. When Debbie was finished, she picked up her pail of soapy water and headed for the door, leaving Anne at the other end of the room. Anne pretended to spill some water on the floor and begged a second to clean it up.

"Hurry up. Meet us in the kitchen when you're finished," said Angela who miraculously left Anne alone in the computer room.

Avoiding the surveillance cameras placed around the room, Anne took the device out of her bra. Using her body to block the cameras, she attached the USB stick to the back of a computer tower underneath the table on the floor. She picked the second to last computer on the left side and slipped it into place even though her hands shook and her body felt on fire.

Then, she quickly picked up her mop and pail and ran out of the room to join the other women in the kitchen. She forced the terrified expression from her face and held her body tight to keep it from shaking.

After the kitchen was cleaned, Angela ushered Debbie and Anne out of the Hartley mansion and into her car. Anne heaved a huge sigh of relief. She was proud that she had achieved her mission but feared discovery. She smiled for the first time when Angela dropped them off at the agency.

That incident with Guenther ran through her aching head, and she worried that her life was in danger. She had slipped invisibly in and out of the mansion successfully. But the USB stick might still give her away.

* * *

When Anne returned to the hotel room, Gary was sitting on the bed smiling brightly. He was so happy to see her. He had been under great stress all day. It wasn't until she was in the computer room and had attached the USB stick to the computer that Gary realized how much danger he was putting his wife in. When she had achieved the impossible, Gary breathed a huge sigh of relief.

From Anne's camera, he printed out a great photograph of Guenther. It showed his scowl from almost tripping over the pail. His eyes were an empty, icy blue.

Gary was able to develop a few other pictures of the interior through his laptop and laser printer. Once he was satisfied that they would be of interest to the group back at Jack's cottage, he forwarded them to Jack's email.

The computer device attached to the Hartley computer would be used to transmit its hard drive to his computer, but it could not be put into use until that evening. Gary didn't want to copy the material while the computers were in use because he didn't wish to be detected. It was obvious from Anne's camera that each person working in that room didn't know what their co-worker was doing. Gary hoped his intrusion would go unnoticed.

With Anne back safe and sound, she and Gary took a leisurely shower to cleanse themselves. Anne was tired from mopping clean floors, and Gary was tired of his endless, rejected telephone inquiries.

Gary did have one good piece of news. He had arranged a lunch with Assistant Secretary Martin Landry of the Bureau of Public Affairs. They agreed to meet on Wednesday at one p.m. at the Melrose Hotel.

Martin Landry was engaged in domestic and international media. He also was involved with security interests which was Gary's main interest in speaking to him. If anyone knew what was going on, Gary believed

Landry did. In addition, if the government complained or commented about the current situation, then they would write to Landry's office. Gary wondered how many emails he had received lately and the nature of their tone.

After the hotel's dinner plates had been removed and the server had vacated the hotel room, Gary sent Jack an email including all of the day's successes. Since things were quiet and going well, he told them he would not contact them tomorrow but promised to write on Wednesday after his meeting with Assistant Secretary Landry.

* * *

Hanging around Jack's computer, the poker buddies and their wives stared at the monitor. They reviewed Tony's email along with the pages of reports transferred from his police detective buddy. They could not believe what they were reading and stood in silence allowing each other to digest the dangerous information.

As they absorbed page after page of police reports describing the disappearance of American citizens, they began to further worry about Anne's close involvement with the Hartley mansion. A quick exchange of looks decided that Anne should leave the cleaning job.

At just that moment, Jack's computer made a bleeping sound announcing that an email had been received. As expected, it was from Gary. They were encouraged by Gary's success in scheduling a personal interview with the Assistant Secretary. They were also happy Anne was able to place the flash drive on the Hartley computer, but they feared she would be discovered.

Jack quickly replied to Gary's email, "You're under the gun. Get out of there!"

"Hopefully he'll follow our advice," said Ted looking up from the computer after the email had been sent.

"I hope so too," agreed Susan, who put her hand on her husband's arm in reassurance.

Jack printed out both Tony's and Gary's emails as well as the police reports and then deleted the files. Nothing should stay on the computer for fear that it could be hacked. Jack showed the group his secret hiding place in the basement behind a bookcase where he would hide the papers.

By the time they gathered in the kitchen, it was just past ten p.m. The children were still outside sitting around a campfire that Jack's sons had built. Peter and Laura's son brought his guitar, and they were singing camp songs.

The parents joined their children and enjoyed the music. They were glad to have an innocent diversion, but all they could think about were Anne and Gary and the danger they were in.

WEDNESDAY

"You know those police reports I gave you?" said Mike to Tony who was sitting across the table at the café.

The men had agreed to meet after Mike had contacted Tony to say that he had new and important information to relay.

"Yeah, sent them to the poker guys," replied Tony.

"Well, two detectives from homicide who gave me that stuff met me last night after work. They're very concerned about what's happening, and they're tired of all the unsolved cases."

"Do they have any idea what's causing the disappearances?"

"No. They couldn't discover who was responsible. No one talked and never any witnesses. No one wanted to bring attention to themselves."

"What are the people saying?"

"The general populace is putting it down to Harold's henchmen but no one can prove their existence."

"I'll pass on the information. Is there anything you guys can do?"

Tony took a sip of coffee, hoping it would warm him up.

"We're teaming up to search for these vanishing people. Any more ideas from your friends in Boston?"

Tony sighed. He hadn't told Mike what Anne's fake documentation was for and wasn't sure he should reveal Anne's infiltration into Harold's mansion. But if something happened to her, it would be good if the police were informed.

"We've got a spy inside. I'm waiting to hear the results. I should know tonight."

Gary had arranged for Tony to take them to the airport for the 9:30 p.m. flight back to Boston.

"Good. Maybe together we'll solve this mess," said Mike finishing up his coffee.

Mike patted Tony on the shoulder then left the table. He dropped his empty coffee cup on the marble counter in easy reach of the coffee house staff, glanced back at Tony still seated at the table, and nodded his head to him.

Tony slowly finished his coffee. He wasn't in any rush today. He had traded shifts with a co-worker so that he could be available for Gary and Anne tonight. He didn't have to start until one p.m. He loved the money his job brought in, but the silence of his passengers was becoming ever more difficult. No one wanted to talk no matter how many conversations he started.

Tony's first fare that day provided some excitement. A couple with a large amount of luggage chatting feverishly. Their destination: the airport. Tony expected a colorful ride.

The happy couple were comfortably dressed in dark blue jeans and a black sweater. They were obviously newly married. Tony thought they were off on their honeymoon until he heard the woman say, "How long do you think we have?"

Her husband whispered, "A week."

Tony strained his ears and closed the window to hear what the young man was saying.

"You didn't tell anyone, did you?" said the husband.

"No one. This secret I kept, but we shouldn't be talking here. We can't trust him," the woman said, nodding at Tony.

"He probably hears everything."

Tony held back a laugh and thought, *I do hear everything*. These two were up to something, and he wanted to help them.

"I'm safe, guys. I can keep my mouth shut."

"Thanks, buddy. Just don't ever tell anyone you took us to the airport," said the young man.

"I promise. My car is clean. You can say whatever you want."

"We're running away," said the young woman.

"Katie!" shouted her husband.

"He's safe, Rob, and it feels good to talk to someone. We've only had each other for so long."

"I know of some people who have run away too," said Tony, looking into the rear view mirror.

"Wow, really?" said Rob. "We didn't know there was anyone else like us."

"Yes. Some people are rebelling. Where are you going?"

"We're going far away from anything Harold," said Katie.

"Well, I wish you both luck," Tony said as he pulled up to the airport's main doors. "Here you go."

"Thanks, buddy," said Rob.

As Rob shook Tony's hand goodbye, he handed him a hundred dollar bill for the ride even though the fare only added to sixty-two dollars. Tony, of course, appreciated the big tip and saluted them as they headed inside the airport.

Just as he started his taxi, a knock sounded at his front right side window. A smartly dressed woman was standing there. Tony acknowledged his empty cab and welcomed the woman into the backseat.

The woman was immaculately dressed in a sea blue skirt and short jacket. A cream-colored blouse rested against her skin. She was attractive but seemed a bit jittery.

"Georgetown," she said to Tony as she closed the taxicab's back door.

Staring at the middle-aged woman in the rear view mirror, Tony noticed she was crying. He didn't know what to say. He wasn't sure whether to try and console her or just keep quiet. The traffic was busy so he decided to keep his eye on the road.

When he glanced back again, the pretty woman's tears had stopped, but she was sniffling. Tony picked up his Kleenex box on the front seat and offered the woman a tissue.

"Want to talk about it?" Tony asked.

"No, not really. If I can't save myself, I just saved my son."

It was obvious what was going on. People were escaping Harold. He drove the attractive but tearful woman to her office in Georgetown and then headed back into the city in the hope of finding new fares.

* * *

Gary and Anne ate breakfast in their cozy hotel room. Anne was dressed in her Harvey Girls' uniform and prepared to leave for work. They kissed and cuddled a bit before Anne was out the door. She wished him luck with his interview, and he reminded her to stay safe. They had received Jack's message and agreed that this would be their last day in D.C.

Anne had to return one more time to retrieve the flash drive she had inserted into the Hartley computer. She had assured Gary that she would have no problem picking up the device and hiding it from the other women. However, Gary still worried for her safety.

As she had done the last three days, Anne boarded the red line Metro to the Hartley Girls agency. She met Debbie on the curb waiting for Angela. They chatted casually as they waited.

"Did you see what Kim Kardashian did last night?" said Debbie.

No, she doesn't interest me, thought Anne, but said, "Missed it. What happened?"

"Oh, it was so exciting . . ." Debbie's happy tirade unfortunately continued for a few minutes before both Debbie and Anne realized that Angela was late. They looked down the street.

"It's really rare for Angela to be late," Debbie said as she rocked on her feet. She put her hand over her eyes and squinted down the road.

"How long have you been working with her?"

"It's been about three months now, and I've had enough. No one likes working with Angela and all the secrecy of that haunted mansion."

Anne saw an opportunity. "Has Angela ever been late before?"

"Not with me. The girls vary every few months. It's like a revolving door. Angela remains but different girls from the agency get stuck with her."

"It seems like an easy enough job. Why do you want to leave?"

"Haven't you noticed how creepy that place is? And Angela is one scary bitch. As long as you keep on her good side, you're fine. But annoy her, and you're looking for another job."

"Well, I'll try to keep on her good side then."

"You're doing a good job so far. You've learned to keep your mouth shut and just do the work."

Finally, the two women noticed Angela's black Accent heading towards them. When the car arrived, Angela waited until both women were in the car before she sped off into traffic. She didn't offer a reason for her tardiness or even speak a word of greeting. There was a mean scowl on her face.

After a couple of minutes, Debbie turned her head sideways and glared at Anne. Her eyes said, *Keep quiet.* Anne nodded and said nothing.

When they reached the Hartley mansion, the women quickly followed Angela into the maintenance room to retrieve their tools. They cleaned the east wing and the rest of the mansion in their usual order. It was another quiet day and the women saw nothing of the inhabitants of the building.

Anne breathed and felt relaxed as she cleaned the place for the last time. She was glad to be rid of this experience.

While the women were in the computer room, Anne maneuvered herself between the computer terminals and the security cameras then removed the USB stick. Anne considered herself lucky that no one noticed. She stuck the device into her bra before standing up to retrieve her pail.

After they finished cleaning the room, the women were approached by the main housekeeper, Flo, who was dressed in a starched grey shirt and tailored white blouse. Her coiffured grey hair was arranged into a bun at the back of her head. Flo nodded at Angela who headed out the back door of the mansion dragging Debbie along with her.

Flo turned to Anne and said, "Come with me."

Anne stared at Angela, who didn't look back. Debbie scrunched her shoulders. She didn't know what was going on. Anne followed Flo across the vestibule into the only room they had never cleaned.

* * *

Seated at the bar in the Melrose Hotel, Gary patiently waited for Martin Landry to arrive. He nervously played with his cell phone and looked over his notes. He didn't have to wait long.

"Hey, Gary," said the Assistant Secretary of the Bureau of Public Affairs. He held out his hand. "Been a while. How have you been?"

Shaking his hand, Gary said, "As well as can be expected these days."

"You aren't recording this conversation, are you?" Landry quickly glanced around the room to see if anyone recognized him.

"I'm not recording."

"If anyone knew I was talking to you, I could lose my job. Everything's crazy at the moment."

"What do you know about the FSC?" said Gary getting right to the point.

"Harold Hartley?"

Gary nodded.

"We know nothing about him. Nothing but a few books and articles he wrote a number of years ago. He vanished from the planet about ten years ago. Now, he has suddenly reappeared."

"I know where he lives and what he's doing."

"What?"

"He's holed up in a large mansion in Bethesda. He's the one who's been collecting all those spy reports."

Landry's mouth hung open. No one in his office had been able to discover anything.

"Do you have any proof?"

"Yes, I've everything you need, but I need to know what you're going to do with it."

"The President, along with his staff, are being blackmailed. They are totally under Hartley's spell. I can't go to any of them."

"My friends and I are completing some research, and we'll forward anything we have."

"Thanks," said Landry. "That will be most helpful."

Gary pushed Landry to reveal something, anything about Harold, but he knew nothing. Realizing that there was no point continuing with the interview, Gary pulled out the secret materials that the guys had collected and handed them to Landry.

Landry rose from the table and inserted Gary's envelope into his briefcase. With a quick look around, he smiled at Gary and made his way out of the hotel bar.

Gary ordered another scotch from the waiter. He had a couple of hours to wait until Anne returned. With the help of the alcohol, he was able to relax a bit. The interview had gone well in his estimation since they had now found someone in the government who was on their side and aware of the situation. Hopefully, Landry would be of further assistance.

After another two drinks, Gary rose and left the bar. He returned to his hotel room to wait for Anne. He checked the airplane's departure, and it was on time. He organized his papers and printed out the plane tickets. He then packed all of their belongings into two small suitcases. Gary made sure everything was ready for when Anne returned so they could leave immediately. He checked the video but Anne had turned it off.

Gary expected Anne at seven-thirty, the time she had returned the last couple of days. Resting uncomfortably on the king-sized bed, he nervously surfed the television channels. He was so stressed from worrying about his wife that he couldn't concentrate. Finally, the news came on at six. He watched with interest.

The news anchors were dressed in grey and blue suits and spoke stiffly. After his experience at the radio station, he knew they feared saying something that would not only jeopardize their jobs but also their lives. The reported news stories dealt with senseless items: the rising price of gas, lost pets, and losses in the stock market. There was no good news or anything of real interest to Gary, so he listened with half an ear while also listening for any sound of Anne's return.

Suddenly, it was eight p.m. The news was long over and Gary hadn't even realized he was watching a sit-com. He glanced at his watch and wondered why Anne was delayed. His anxiety level climbed. He checked Anne's camera again. It was still off.

Gary telephoned Tony.

"I'm on my way," Tony said.

"Anne still hasn't returned."

"I'll call you when I reach the hotel."

"Thanks, Tony. I'll see you then."

Slowly pacing the hotel room, Gary looked at his watch every few minutes. He couldn't understand why Anne was so late. She knew they were to take the nine-thirty flight out of D.C. He became increasingly anxious.

Thirty minutes later, Tony phoned Gary from the curb in front of the Marriott hotel.

"Could you wait?" asked Gary. "Anne's still not here."

"Of course," Tony replied and moved his taxi over to the end of the pick-up line.

He left the vehicle and told the doorman that he was waiting for someone in the hotel. The doorman waved Tony off and allowed him to remain where he was.

Fifteen minutes later, Gary retrieved their luggage and met Tony in his car.

"She's not back," Gary cried out as soon as Tony lowered his window.

"Can you call her?" offered Tony as he got out of the taxi.

"There's no way to reach her. She didn't take her cell phone and the camera is off. I don't know what to do."

"You should get out of D.C. Let the police take over."

"I can't leave Anne."

"You have no real choice. If you attempted some sort of a rescue, you might just put your wife in further danger."

"Yes, I know. Damn it, I can't even contact Anne's agency. Can I give you their number? Could your police friends contact them?"

"Yes, of course. Don't worry. We'll find your wife, but first we have to get you to safety. Go back to your friends."

Gary grumbled and stomped his feet. "I know you're right, but I can't leave D.C."

Tony put his hand on Gary's back. "Get in the car and I'll drive you to the airport."

Reluctantly, Gary slid into the backseat, and they took off into traffic. After a quick drive, Tony reached the airport. He turned around and addressed his unhappy fare.

"I'll contact Mike immediately. Don't worry. We'll find your wife."

"Thanks, Tony."

Collecting his few belongings, Gary slowly made his way into the airport. He had missed his flight but was lucky enough to get an empty seat on the ten-thirty flight.

Once Gary finished with security, he found a quiet corner of the airport near his gate and telephoned the guys at the cottage.

"What do you mean she's disappeared?" said Ruth who had picked up the phone.

"She didn't return from work. I'm at the airport. Tony said he would get his police friend to locate her. I'm debating about leaving D.C."

"Come back immediately," said Jack who took the phone from his wife. "It's too dangerous."

"Fine. I'll leave, but I'm not happy about it," Gary said just as his boarding announcement sounded.

After Jack hung up the phone, he called everyone into the living room and passed on the news.

"I knew this was too dangerous," Susan said, falling into a chair.

"No point discussing that now. We need to find Anne," said Laura. She sat down on the couch beside her husband.

Jack paced. He stopped in the center of the room and declared confidently, "Tony's friend will help."

"We can't do anything from here. We'll just have to wait. Come on everyone. Let's cheer up for Gary. He's going to be a mess when he arrives," said Susan, who didn't like the tension in the room.

By midnight, the children were in bed, and the adults were settled in the living room having a much-needed drink. When a car pulled up, the men ran out the front door.

Gary's golf shirt and jeans were ruffled, his hair needed a brush, and his face was worn. But he tried to smile when he saw his friends. He didn't know what to

193

say to Renee. She was sleeping so he could wait to handle that problem in the morning.

As soon as Gary entered the cottage, all his friends jostled around him.

"She returned to the hotel every night by seven-thirty. She never faltered from that time," he blurted out desperate to talk with his friends.

"Had she noticed anything?" Ted asked, coming to stand beside him. "I mean, did she suspect she was in any danger?"

"No. She never saw anyone from the mansion and no one ever saw her, except Guenther who bumped into her once but I doubt he'd remember her."

"Did she do anything that would have brought her to anyone's attention?" asked Mark. He guided the group to the living room.

"Nothing. No wait. She placed the flash drive on one of the Hartley computers. She was retrieving it today."

"They must have seen her," Mark said. He pushed Gary onto the couch between Ruth and Susan. "There were lots of surveillance cameras around, right?"

"Do you think that was it?" cried Gary. "Did I kill my wife?"

"It's not your fault," Peter said, as he put his arms around Laura.

"No, it's not," said Ruth. She put her arm around Gary, and he leaned into her.

"Looks like we need a new dealer," said Mark, sitting down in a chair.

"She must have been seen inserting my programmed USB stick. Damn! Why did I have her do that? I just didn't think. When Anne told me that she cleaned that room, all I could think about was getting into those computers." Gary dropped his head into his hands and let out a scream. Ruth and Susan patted him on the back.

"I don't mean to change the subject, but did you get the computer files?" said Jack.

"Yes, I did," said Gary. "I've only glanced at them. Here, take my laptop and check them out for yourselves. I'm too tired now."

Gary handed his laptop to Jack.

"Go to bed," Ruth said. "We'll take it from here."

"Thanks. I think I will."

He walked up the stairs to the bedroom he and Anne shared. Gary needed time to think of what to say to his daughter in the morning.

Back in the living room, Jack turned on Gary's laptop and found the secret files. Opening up the main Hartley segment, a list of every city was revealed. In each city were the names of every adult with a number from one through five beside the name.

Most names had a one or two. There were a few threes and fours, but they were rare. Only after digging deeper did they notice names with a five.

The group brain stormed the meaning of the numbers. Finally, after a little digging, they found their own names. A four was next to each of them.

"Check this out," said Mark and he grabbed the laptop from Jack. "I reviewed those police reports that Constable Mike sent us. Look at this."

Turning to the last person on the list with a five beside their name, Mark then held up the police report with the same man's name on it. This man had disappeared over a month ago.

Double clicking on the man's name in the Hartley file, Mark displayed this man's whole life. The group read all about Keith Joseph, a thirty-four year old civil rights lawyer, living in New York City. He had a long time live-in girlfriend, who was also an attorney but in corporate law. Photographs of both individuals were contained in the file. At the bottom of the biography was a notation: disruptive force.

Keith's misdeeds were noted in the file: wearing ties too flamboyant, not attending church as charged by Harold's laws, challenging the FSC mission to spy on his neighbor. He had failed to send in the reports.

Laura pointed out the section where Keith approached the *New York Times* to detail his dissent and displeasure with the FSC, but the newspaper wouldn't print such an article.

The last notation in Keith's file was the number five and the words "to be terminated."

Scrolling down the Hartley list, Mark saw a few more fives. While everyone else went to bed, Mark stayed up all night going through the whole Hartley file and listed all the people who had the number four or five beside their names.

It was four in the morning by the time Mark completed the task. In the end, he had a list of seventy-eight names of people who had the words "to be terminated" listed at the bottom of their file. Mark then compared the fives to the missing or dead people in the police reports. He was able to match seventy-four names.

He made a separate list of all the names and cities of the people who were either dead or missing, which he put into an email and forwarded directly to Tony to hand over to his detective friend.

Just after six a.m., Mark crawled into bed beside Maggie, who was fast asleep. Mark took her into his arms and pulled her close. They had been developing a deep relationship while hiding in Jack's cottage. He loved the way Maggie had slipped easily into their lives. She mixed well with the wives and didn't seem to mind the hoard of children. He had finally found the right woman with whom to share his life.

THURSDAY

Outside the coffee house, Tony waited for Mike with two coffees in his hands. When Mike arrived, he said, "Let's walk."

"What's up?" asked Mike, accepting one of the coffees.

"Something has happened and we need your help," said Tony said as he handed Mike a few papers.

"Anne Martin has gone missing. She went undercover, under the name of Anne Patterson, as a cleaning woman in the Hartley mansion. She didn't return last night."

"That's the woman I got the fake documents for?"

"Yes," said fearing Mike's response.

Mike didn't say a word but glanced at the papers Tony had handed him. He paused at the photograph of Anne in her Harvey Girls' outfit. She was a pleasant-looking woman with mousey brown hair but bright grey eyes. Gary had taken the picture before Anne left on her first day on the job.

Amongst the pages was the contract with the Harvey Girls as well as a copy of her hours. The names of all the women Anne had contact with since attending at the Harvey Girls Agency were also listed.

"I'll look into this immediately," said Mike.

"We have to find her."

"Okay, off I go. I'll call you once I have any news."

Mike crossed the street, leaving Tony alone on the sidewalk. While in his vehicle, Mike reviewed the papers again. His first step would be to interview the manager at the Harvey Girls agency. Mike started his engine and drove the few blocks to the office building.

Parking near the front doors, Mike left his car and made his way into the tall, glass building. He found a pretty, young girl dressed in a green-flowered dress sitting in the receptionist's position. He showed his badge and asked to see her manager.

The receptionist quickly picked up the telephone and called her boss to say that a police officer was waiting.

Once the call had been completed, the girl asked Mike to sit. "June Brooks will attend you shortly."

Taking a seat on one of the comfortable chairs, Mike picked up a brochure about the agency's business. He read how the Harvey Girls provided cleaning services for any location. Nothing was too small or too big for them to clean. The women in the pamphlet appeared happy and enthusiastic in their starched, grey uniforms. Mike slipped a copy into his briefcase just as a well-dressed woman in her forties walked towards him.

"Hello, Officer. I'm June Brooks. Can I help you?"

June was an attractive older woman, who obviously dyed her gray hair to a honey-brown shade. Her dark blue skirt and jacket attire were simple yet elegant.

"Yes," said Mike. "Perhaps we could talk in your office?"

"That's fine. Please follow me."

June lead Mike through a large room full of cubicles in which a number of women were facing a computer screen. Some glanced nervously at him while he passed by their stations.

Once inside June's office, Mike closed the door behind him and sat down at the offered chair in front of her black wood desk. June gracefully planted herself into her soft pastel office chair.

"I'm looking for one of your employees," said Mike.

"Which one?"

"Anne Patterson," said Mike, using her assumed name. "She joined your agency last week. She didn't return home last night. Do you have any information about her?"

"Let me look. I don't remember that name."

June turned to the computer on her desk. She took the mouse in hand and moved it around the pad, clicking here and there. Finally, she lifted her head from the computer and stared straight at Mike. "We don't have a woman by that name working for us."

"That's impossible. I have a contract here which states that Anne Patterson was named an employee of the Harvey Girls."

Mike pulled out the copied form from his briefcase and handed it to June, carefully watching her face.

But June's facial features showed no expression. She handled the contract as if it burned her fingers. She made some comment that these things can be falsified. She was sure this contract was a fake.

"I also have her hours which she provided to you at the end of each work day."

Mike held out a piece of paper with two weeks full of dates and numbers.

"I'm sorry. But I have no confirmation of this," said June who barely glanced at the paper.

Not about to give up, he asked, "May I speak to Angela and Debbie?"

"I have no way of reaching them during the work day. Debbie has to enter her work hours and so she will be here once her day has been completed. You can speak to her then. I can provide you with Angela's cell phone number, but she is difficult to reach."

"Would you please arrange an appointment with her?"

"I suppose I could leave a message and let her contact you."

"That's just not good enough. It's urgent that I speak with her. I will contact her directly?"

June whispered, "I'll speak to Angela after work."

"Is there anything else you can do for me?" said Mike with an optimistic tone, hoping for some admission.

"I have nothing more to tell you."

Rising from the stiff office chair, Mike turned and left June's office without saying another word. He was sure he was being deceived even though he couldn't prove it.

Obviously, June was lying about hiring Anne. He could tell when people were lying to him. He suspected that Anne's whole history with the Harvey Girls had been wiped clean from their computers. There was no point in trying to obtain a subpoena. He would find nothing.

He must find the answers from Angela Barrett. He had no information about her other than that she drove a 2014 black Hyundai Accent, license number 9BB G52. He pulled her driving record from his police computer. It was clean. No one is that perfect. Everyone gets a ticket for something. This warranted further scrutiny.

Making his way up to his office, Mike ventured first to homicide to search for his mates, Allan Palmer and Chuck Stocker. Both men looked similar in appearance with short brown hair and brown eyes, but that is where the comparison ended. Allan was a flamboyant Jewish man, who loved clothes and was always dressed in three-piece suits. Chuck was a Catholic Irishman, who preferred to be more conservatively dressed in black jeans, white undershirt, and blue long-sleeved shirt.

Over the past few months, Chuck and Allan had only run into brick walls at the police department. They had attempted to find people to stand up against Harold, but no one would agree to discuss it. When Mike had come to them, they were pleased to help hoping this new connection would bring them closer to stopping Harold.

The partners shared an office, and Mike walked straight in, quickly closing their door behind him. "We have a big mystery on our hands, and I need your help."

"Sure, Mike. Sit down and tell us what we can do," said Chuck who turned away from his laptop to face Mike.

"A woman who went undercover as a house cleaner at the Hartley's mansion has disappeared. She did not return from work yesterday and the agency doesn't seem to have any record of her."

"Do you have a missing person's report?" asked Allan.

"No, this is a private request," said Mike.

"Any leads?" said Chuck.

"I'll be meeting with an Angela Barrett who drove our woman to work every day. Here's her driving record. See what you can find out about her."

"We can do that," said Allan.

He picked up the paper with Angela's information and glanced at it then handed it to his partner, who took his time reading it over.

"Thanks guys. Fast as you can, please. We have to find her."

Allan and Chuck smiled at Mike as he left their office.

Mike made his way up to his own office on the sixth floor. A pile of files lay on the top of his desk. These all dealt with the missing or dead people. He put aside his paperwork to read over those police reports.

He organized the files into two piles: dead and missing people. There were seventy-eight folders of dead people and another twenty recently missing people from all over the U.S. He read through and made notes. He tried to figure out what they had in common, but he could see no similarities. Scrutinizing the papers, he attempted to discover anything about them.

The diligence of the dead people's spies was apparent. Everything about the victims had been recorded. In none of the descriptions were any mention of attending a church. In addition, at the bottom of each page, it was noted that they were not mailing in their spy reports. Obviously, this was enough to terminate their lives. All the dead people's reports showed the same notations.

Turning to the files of the missing people, he read over their reports, seeking to find something that could connect them to each other or the dead people. He spent hours going over those papers but found nothing similar except for the fact that all of the people were in one way or another atheists. None of their files mentioned any church or place of worship.

His laptop made a startling ring, informing him that an email had been received. It was from the cabbie, Tony. It seemed that Tony's friends in Boston had tapped into Harold's computer system. They had discovered seventy-eight people with a five beside their name, a number that correlated with the police files of the dead people. They had also figured out that any person with a number five beside their name was to be killed.

Mike printed out the email and returned to the files on the deceased individuals. Yes, there it was. All the dead people on the police reports were listed as being number five on Harold's report. He then looked over the missing files and, again, the names correlated with Tony's friends' list. With the twenty missing person's files, he made notes of their locations and times of disappearance.

Taking the most recent disappearance first, Mike phoned the local police department in that area, and talked to the detective on the case. The policeman described the missing person as an average man with no outstanding characteristics.

"I spoke with his wife. She was terrified to talk with me. They were of no help," said the detective.

"May I have her phone number? I'd like to give her a call," said Mike.

"Sure."

The detective read aloud the woman's number and address. Mike copied down this information directly onto the missing man's file.

Mike asked, "Do you have any other files of mysterious disappearances or suspicious deaths?"

The detective listed a couple, which Mike already had on his desk. He asked for the home phone numbers for the spouses or partners of those missing people. He then thanked the detective, and hung up.

Mike contacted each of the missing person's families. Each relayed the same material: their spouse had gone to work and not returned home. There was nothing special about any of the cases.

Then Mike thought to ask, "What religion do you follow?"

The other end of the line became silent. Then a coughing sound was heard along with some mumbling.

"Could you speak a little clearer?" Mike asked.

It was then he finally received the important information he required. Each of the missing person's family was non-religious. Most were atheists and would not attend any kind of church. Since the family member had disappeared, the rest of the family had begun attending church. They wouldn't expand on their religious beliefs.

After the phone calls had been concluded, Mike again reviewed the list of Americans that Tony had sent. He circled those few names for which there were no police reports. The number four was beside each of those names.

He printed the names of people in danger and called each police department in those cities. The policemen were not exactly thrilled with the idea of warning someone in danger. Mike had to persuade them to visit the person's home and warn them in person. Finally, after much persuasion and cajoling, Mike convinced the police officers to follow his advice. He asked them to report back to him with any important details.

Once that ordeal had been completed, Mike looked at the time and willed himself out of his office and into a restaurant down the street for dinner. While waiting for his meal to be delivered, he phoned Tony.

"You're calling late," Tony said. "Been at it all day?"

"Yes. Thanks for your email. I have police officers on the trail of those who have not as yet disappeared but are on your friends' list. Would it be possible to contact them directly?"

"I'll pass along your message. How about I give them your number and have one of them call you."

"Sure. Fine," said Mike. "Dinner's here. Talk to you later," and Mike hung up the phone.

Immediately, Tony texted Mark about Mike's interest to talk to them. He could do no more.

FRIDAY

While at the dinner table, Mark received a text from Tony. He transferred the message that Constable Mike wished to personally communicate with them.

"I'm not sure that's wise," said Mark, putting down his phone.

Placing his fork and knife on the plate, Ted said, "We could use all the help we can get."

"Can we trust him?" asked Peter, finishing off the roast chicken.

"He's a police officer," said Ruth.

"That doesn't mean anything these days," Mark said.

"Yes, I agree," said Jack.

"Should we take the chance?" asked Susan, collecting the dirty dishes.

"I think we should," said Ted. "We can't proceed any further alone and we need help rescuing Anne."

"Okay," said Mark, deciding for the group. "I'll call Mike now."

After a few rings, a deep, low voice said, "Constable Mike Verns."

"Hello, Constable Verns. This is Mark Wadley speaking. That Boston friend of Tony's."

"Oh hey. Thanks for calling."

"Did Tony pass along our findings?"

"Yes. Thanks. That Hartley list corresponded well with our police files. You know those that weren't reported on?"

"Yeah."

"I've organized some good cops to visit them. Hopefully, they'll be in time to warn them of impending danger."

"Glad to have been of assistance. Have you had any luck finding Anne?"

"I have two fine officers on the case. Should hear something by tomorrow."

"Good. The sooner the better."

Reading Jack's lips, Mark asked, "What did the Harvey Girls agency say about Anne?"

Mike explained how he had met with the branch manager and that she had obviously lied. "That's a dead end."

Holding the phone aside for a second, Mark told the group this latest bit of information.

"Can he get hold of their files?" asked Peter.

"I'll ask," said Mark.

"There's no point," replied Mike. "I'm sure she has deleted any mention of Anne from their records."

"I'll get back to you as soon as possible."

"It's all my fault," Gary moaned after Mark hung up the phone.

"No, it isn't," said Susan, putting a hand on his shoulder.

"It wasn't your fault," agreed Jack. "We needed those records. You were right to ask Anne to place that flash drive. Look at what we've accomplished."

"But look at the price we've had to pay," cried Ruth.

"The police will find Anne. I'm sure of it," said Laura.

"I hope you're right," said Gary.

Rising suddenly from the dinner table, Gary knocked over his chair and left, climbing the stairs to his bedroom to lie down. This new information upset him terribly and his body ached. He had to be alone with his misery. Once in his bedroom, he threw himself onto the bed. With his face in the pillow, he cried tears of anger. Would he ever see Anne again?

SATURDAY

As soon as Mike reached his office, he turned on his computer and found the expected email from Allan and Chuck, the police officers helping him to locate Anne. The email detailed their work in uncovering Angela Barrett. They provided him with her address and home phone number. She had moved to Washington, D.C. three years ago when she began working for the Harvey Girls agency. Although Allan and Chuck had diligently researched her past, they couldn't pick up her trail beyond three years ago. She seems to have just suddenly appeared.

Mike was dying to speak to her. He had so many unanswered questions. Since it was Saturday, he expected her to be at home.

Angela's address wasn't a great distance so Mike decided to pay her a visit. After a short drive, he marched up her front steps and knocked loudly on the front door. He noticed someone moving within the house. Just as he was about to knock again, the door opened a crack.

"Can I help you?" said the woman behind the door.

"Are you Angela Barrett?"

"Yes. Who are you?"

"Constable Verns from the Washington Police Department. I have a few questions to ask you."

"I'm sorry, but I'm on my way out. Could we meet another time?"

"No. Right now is fine. May I come in?" said Mike as he prepared to enter the house.

Opening the door a little wider, but not wide enough to allow him to enter, Angela said, "Here is just fine."

"So be it."

Mike pulled out his notepad and began the interview.

"Do you know this woman?" said Mike as he pulled out a photograph of Anne Martin.

"Never saw her before," said Angela without missing a beat.

"You don't know this woman, Anne Patterson?" said Mike, using Anne's alias.

"Never heard of her."

"You work for the Harvey Girls Agency?"

"Yes."

"For how long?"

"Three years."

"Your present employment requires you to clean the home at 320 Sycamore Avenue, Bethesda?"

"Yes, that's correct."

"Any details you would like to provide would be most appreciated."

Angela stood stiffly staring blankly at him in her long, pink robe. She held tightly to the edge of the door.

"I understand that every day you pick up two cleaning women and the three of you drive to the

Hartley mansion," said Mike changing the subject yet again.

"Yes."

Mike glanced at Angela and noted her discomfort. He was getting to her but he wasn't sure she would break.

"What do you know about the inhabitants of the Hartley place?"

"Nothing. I just clean."

"So, you've never seen or heard of Anne Patterson," said Mike.

"No. Never. I've answered your questions. You can see I am of no help to you. Would you please leave and let me carry on with my day?"

"Fine. Here's my card. Call me if you come across anything," said Mike.

She slammed the door on Mike who had learned nothing to assist him. It was obvious that Angela was lying to him but he couldn't beat out the truth from her as much as he would have liked to. He retraced his steps to his police vehicle and was soon on his way back to the police station.

* * *

"A cop spoke to Ms. Barrett this morning," said Guenther, who stood before Harold in his study.

"Who's Ms. Barrett?" said Harold, yawning loudly.

213

"The cleaning woman."

"Why bother me with such petty matters? You know what to do."

Harold barely noticed Guenther. He sat behind the Monster and seemed preoccupied with shuffling the papers on his desk. Guenther, realizing the situation, turned on his heel and left the room closing the door behind him.

Ian glared at his brother in shock. "Is that necessary?"

"Yes, it is and you shouldn't bother yourself with such things," said Harold.

"What about the police?"

"The police are no problem. I've taken care of them. Just worry about the money."

"I wish you would hire an accountant. I spend many unnecessary hours with the books because I don't know what I'm doing."

"Learn," ordered Harold.

"It's really too difficult for me. You have money coming in from so many places. It's hell trying to keep up with it all."

"Stop whining and do the work!"

Knowing he should say nothing further, Ian bowed his head. His brother returned to staring at the computer screen. Ian then realized that his brother had never taken his eyes off the screen while talking to him, annoying Ian to no end. Harold rarely made eye contact.

Ian stepped out of Harold's study, slamming the door behind him, a defiant gesture that Harold didn't even notice.

Ian worried about that woman kept hostage in the attic. He wondered if she was the spouse of one of the men who had taken him hostage. She would be kept captive until Harold decided what to do with her.

Rarely did Ian have anything to do with the cleaning staff. That was Flo's job. A couple of times, he did run into the women but never paid them much attention. He had recognized Angela since she had been cleaning the mansion for so many years, but he had never spoken to her. Now, she too would be taken prisoner.

Feeling the matter was urgent, Ian had to speak to the captive woman to try and discover something about her. Harold wouldn't approve and this act could get him into some considerable trouble. Still, Ian decided to keep an ear out for a time when he could sneak up to the attic and interview Anne.

The only information Anne had given them was her name. She wouldn't betray anything else. Franz was going to take care of that. Anne didn't seem like a very tough woman and Harold was sure she would reveal all when pressured. Ian shuddered at the thought that she would be harmed.

Crossing the spacious vestibule, Ian stepped into the War Room. The employees were busy entering all that data into the computers, data which Harold studied for hours.

On the counter was a black file folder filled with pieces of white paper. The slips of paper accounted for every single penny that came in or went out of the mansion. He gathered up this material and left the room to walk down the hallway to his office. It was not as extravagant as his brother's, but it was where Ian felt most at home. It had been his mother's making it special to him.

Ian's study held every book he had ever read. Every novel by Charles Dickens was there along with Mark Twain, Ernest Hemingway, Kurt Vonnegut, Thomas Hardy, and F. Scott Fitzgerald. All those titles now lay on built-in wooden, cherry wood bookcases.

On the wall spaces between the bookcases hung dramatic landscape paintings. Bold colors and strong strokes showed off lightning strikes and deadly cloud formations. Ian was a great art lover and he had collected a few paintings created by the sensational American artist William Merritt Chase.

These original paintings featured different aspects of Central Park, New York. Ian treasured these paintings. His first routine every day was to dust his paintings and bookshelves.

Retrieving the black folders, Ian organized the files into different colored trays on his desk. This was a system devised by his mother. Each color represented a different expense coming in or out. Once all the papers were in their appropriate places, Ian turned on his computer and began to enter all the information into the appropriate sections of the accounting program.

While entering the numbers, Ian's mind drifted off and he thought about Harold. Three years his senior, Harold began his Master's Degree in Biochemistry the year Ian entered college. Chemical torture was the topic for Harold's doctoral degree. Harold seemed mainly interested in figuring out how people tick and finding ways to take them apart. He was not always successful, however, in putting people together again.

Even though the brothers studied in the same building at Georgetown, they rarely spent much time together. Ian only saw his brother during the traditional Sunday night meal in the Hartley mansion.

As Ian worked the books, he realized that a lot of money was coming into the mansion and he couldn't understand why. No one had told him of any new donations but here they were and from individuals in amounts ranging from $100 to thousands of dollars. Their names had no meaning to him and he was too scared to ask Harold about it. Grumbling, Ian just completed his job to the best of his ability.

When he finally finished, his thoughts turned to Anne and his decision about talking to her. Maybe he could break the woman. It was worth a shot.

SUNDAY

The breakfast dishes had been cleaned and put away. Everything in the kitchen was in its proper place and the room was spotless. The children were outside enjoying the great sunny warm weather. Their parents had given them another challenge: to make sparks with a foil pie plate, pan, tack, wool sock, Styrofoam, and glue. After putting these things together and rubbing the sock against the Styrofoam, a spark or lightening could be seen.

While the kids were pre-occupied, the poker buddies and their wives came together in the living room to decide their next step.

"This is what we know," said Jack, summing up their situation for everyone. "Tony's police friend Mike is on our side and has put two policemen he can trust on Anne's trail. We have that man Gary contacted in the Bureau of Public Affairs. However, we still need to give them some hard evidence."

"What about kidnapping Guenther?" said Gary. His tired face showed the strain and stress of losing Anne. He was out for blood now.

"We could do that," said Mark, settling himself on the couch beside Ruth.

"Wouldn't that be dangerous?" said Ruth, patting Mark on the leg.

"Possibly," said Jack. "But what have we got to lose. We're on the button. Let's pick him up when he leaves the post office."

"He might be armed," said Peter, holding up his hand for attention.

"We have to take that chance," Ted said. He picked up his wife's hand and kissed it.

"Why don't we get Tony to watch the Hartley mansion again," said Jack.

"What will that do?" asked Peter.

"Find out if anything's different. Maybe learn something new?" said Jack.

"Not a bad idea," said Laura. She shrugged her shoulders as the other woman stared at her.

"I'll call Tony," said Mark. "I told him I'd be calling this morning."

It took a while for Tony to answer his phone.

On the sixth ring, Tony said, "Sorry, could you hold a sec?"

Mark said, "Sure," and he waited.

Once Tony returned to the phone, he said, "Sorry, Mark. I've got lots of news."

"Do tell."

"That woman Angela, who drove Anne to work, has disappeared. Also, we've learned that there's no past information about her. Do you have a picture of her?"

Holding the cell phone away from his ear, Mark put the question to Gary, who said he would be able to get something off the video Anne took. Gary opened his laptop and searched for a good picture of Angela. When he found a sufficient representation, he emailed the photo to Tony's cell phone.

"Okay," said Mark to Tony. "Gary just sent you a picture of Angela."

"Constable Mike has policemen on the trail of those people on Hartley's list who have a four or five by their name. He hopes to save them before they disappear."

"That's great. I hope they're successful. Anything else we can do?"

"No. Constable Mike thinks it is best that you just lay low for the time being."

"That we can do."

"I'll call you tomorrow," said Tony as he hung up the phone.

"I do so hope the police reach those people in time," said Susan after Mark relayed the news.

"They should," said Jack, patting Susan's arm.

"So, we're still going to capture Guenther, right?" asked Gary.

"Yes, I think we should," said Jack, crossing his arms.

"Should we warn Mike what we're doing?" Peter said.

"No, not until we have Guenther. Then, we can turn him over to the police. We have to find Anne first and have proof against Harold," said Ted.

"I agree," said Mark. "I think we should buy our airplane tickets separately. We shouldn't sit together."

"Good idea," agreed Jack. "Where do we take him?"

"Maggie, can we use your place again?" asked Mark.

"Sure," said Maggie. She ran to her bedroom and rummaged through her purse to find her house keys.

The men brought out their laptops and each made a reservation for the eight a.m. flight to D.C. They hoped to have further information about Anne by then.

* * *

Ian crept up to the attic. He had avoided Flo after sending her off on an errand. Everyone else was busy working and wouldn't notice Ian's meanderings. He maneuvered himself around the surveillance cameras making it look like he was just harmlessly wandering around.

When he reached the attic, Ian heaved a huge sigh of relief. He put a handkerchief on the camera pointed at Anne's room so no one would see him going in. Slowly he strode up to a door and put a key in the lock. When he opened the door, he found Anne sleeping on the bed.

Feeling a stir in the air, Anne woke up startled to see Ian in the room. She seemed to recognize him and he gathered that could only be possible if she was the spouse of one of the kidnappers. She moved to a sitting position covering her body with the blanket.

"What do you want?" she whispered.

"I need to talk to you."

"About what?"

"I was kidnapped by some men. Are you a spouse of one?"

Anne went white but said nothing.

"I won't hurt you but you have to be honest with me?"

"Why?"

"I could save your life."

Anne brought her legs up to her chin and held them tight. "Is my life in danger?"

"Yes," Ian said as he moved closer to the bed.

Anne gazed at him up and down, then asked, "Are you Ian Hartley?"

Feeling uncomfortable, Ian said, "So you know who I am."

"Yes, I do." Anne looked him in the eye then lowered her head.

"So your husband did kidnap me?"

Anne kept her eyes down and rested her head upon her knees.

"Tell me the truth," Ian demanded but Anne said nothing.

Frustrated, Ian backed out of the room, locked the door, then removed the cloth from the surveillance camera once he was out of its view. He made his way back to his office angry that she hadn't confided in him. He didn't care now if she lived or died.

* * *

Allan picked up the ringing phone, "Homicide."

"Hey Allan. It's Mike. What you got for me?"

"Sorry, Mike. I wish we had more, but this Angela woman is a ghost. She arrived in D.C. three years ago from who knows where. She just appeared out of the blue. We contacted the previous owners of Angela's house and they said she paid in cash. Her driver's license is clean. She bought her car from a dealer in town and, again, paid cash."

"Well that's something. Anything else?"

"We have a warrant before the judge to allow us to enter the Hartley mansion. It's been sitting on his desk all day, and we have yet to hear. This could take a while."

"It's a start. Stick with that and let me know the outcome as soon as possible."

TUESDAY

The poker buddies' adventure was finally organized, and they had decided to bring Constable Mike into their plans. They would meet at Maggie's townhouse where Mike could interrogate Guenther. Mark had given Mike their flight schedule in case something went wrong.

They had discussed different possible methods in which to capture Guenther. The best solution was for Jack and Mark, the biggest and the strongest of the five, to wait for Guenther beside his silver SUV. They would grab him, drag him into the van where Peter and Gary would then take control of him while they drove to Maggie's home. Everything was perfectly planned.

It was decided that Ted would drive this time and the rest of the guys would sit in the back. After picking up the dark blue van at the airport, Ted drove to the post office. Peter pointed out Guenther's car parked across the street.

Ted pulled up just behind Guenther's silver SUV and they waited. They kept their eyes focused on the front doors of the post office building. Once in a while, someone would make a comment about someone they saw, but they kept their minds on the goal.

After what seemed like forever, the poker buddies watched as Guenther left the post office. He carried two large valises. From the staggered way he walked, it was obvious those bags were heavy. He didn't seem interested in anything but reaching his car.

Ted turned on the ignition. As soon as Guenther came alongside his SUV, Ted quickly pulled out from behind his car to rest beside it. When Mark pulled open the side door, Guenther was found standing in the perfect place just outside the door. He turned his head and noticed the men. His face turned white and his eyes grew large. He dropped the valises with a thud.

Not giving him a chance to get away, Jack jumped out of the van and grabbed his body. He threw both arms around him and held him tight. Guenther, recovering from the shock, thrashed around attempting to break Jack's grip but Jack was stronger than him.

Next out of the van was Mark who seized Guenther's flailing arms and brought them together. With one hand, he slapped handcuffs on his hands. Then he patted him down looking for a weapon, which he found in his belt. He handed the gun to Gary.

Jack and Mark then dragged Guenther into the open van. Guenther kicked his legs and squirmed in their tight grasp but he was no match for the two men. He tried to scream but Mark put his hand over his mouth.

Once inside the van, Peter bound his mouth so he wouldn't be able to speak. Gary attached Guenther's seatbelt. When everything was secure, Ted pulled out into traffic, leaving Guenther's SUV behind.

It was a slow drive because of heavy traffic. The men spoke to each other with their eyes. They had agreed to stay silent until they reached Maggie's house.

Guenther wrestled against the handcuffs, but his bonds were tight. He tried yelling, but his cries were muffled.

When they finally reached Maggie's townhouse, the poker buddies spied Mike's police vehicle resting by the stone curb out in front. When Mike saw the van pull up, he exited his car and marched up to the front door to await the men.

Mark opened the door of the van and took one of Guenther's arms. Gary took the other and half-walked, half-dragged him into Maggie's townhouse. Once on the top step, Mike swiftly opened the front door and moved immediately into the living room. Ted closed the curtains and put a chair in the middle of the room for Guenther who was obviously angry at being captured.

The men took up positions around the living room. Once everyone was prepared, Ted removed the cloth from around Guenther's mouth.

Guenther spat, "How dare you! You fuckers! You're dead men."

The men chuckled and passed the baton to Mike who pulled out a pad of paper listing questions for the belligerent Guenther. Only Mike would be speaking.

"Are you Guenther Baskilin?" asked Mike.

"Who wants to know?"

"American citizens," said Mike.

"You aren't the police. The police don't kidnap people. Take this fuckin' thing off my head," Guenther demanded.

"I'm sorry," said Mike, smiling at the guys. "We can't do that. Either you tell me your name or we'll check your pockets for your wallet. Your choice."

Guenther pursed his lips and said nothing.

"We want the truth," said Mike, who wasn't going to allow Guenther's angry demeanor to influence him or his questions.

"The truth about what?"

"Who you are and your relationship to Harold."

Guenther shook his head and said nothing.

"C'mon, Guenther. We know you're working for him."

Guenther struggled trying to break out of his bonds but they held him fast. He kicked out his legs as if he was trying to reach someone but the guys moved out of range. Finally, he tried to lose the blindfold.

"You're dead men," growled Guenther.

"Well, that's only possible if you can find us." Mike decided to try a different tactic. "We know you're holding two women captive."

Guenther's body stiffened and he sat erect in the chair.

"So you are holding Anne and Angela Barrett?" Mike moved to stand in front of Guenther.

"I don't know what you are talking about." Guenther puffed out his chest.

"Are both women alive?" Mike looked at Gary.

"I don't know what you are talking about," Guenther repeated. "Never heard of those women."

Mike tapped him on the shoulder and said, "What would we find if we searched Harold's home?"

"There's no way you'll be allowed on the property. That's an empty threat." Guenther leaned back sticking his chin in the air.

Mike didn't want to reveal their work to obtain a search warrant so he decided to return to questioning him about Harold. "What's Harold planning?"

"Ask him."

"Can you set up an interview?"

"You've got to be kidding." Guenther let out a bold snicker. "He's a god, and you're nothing. Why would he lower himself to speak with you?"

"But you can talk to me. What's your purpose in the organization?" asked Mike.

Guenther pursed his lips.

"What's Harold's purpose?" Mike pushed.

Guenther licked his lips then said, "He's achieved his purpose."

Looks of shock registered on the faces of the men.

"What has he achieved?"

"Proven he's God."

The men burst out laughing causing Guenther to scowl.

"There's a force against him," said Mike defiantly.

"We're taking care of them."

"The fives?"

Shocked, Guenther's body became rigid. He stopped talking and sat still barely moving. Mike bet he wondered how they knew about Harold's numbering system.

"You've just signed Anne's death warrant."

Guenther had put two and two together, and realized that Anne had stolen the computer files which Gary had hacked.

Gary almost fainted when he realized that Anne was still alive. Ted, who was sitting next to Gary on the couch, put his arm around him. All eyes were on Gary while a collective sigh was uttered. Guenther realized that he had unintentionally divulged an important piece of information.

Not allowing the heavy silence to continue, Mike said, "Where is Anne being held?"

"Nowhere you could find her!"

"You'll lead us to her."

"I'm not letting you in the mansion."

Mike caught Gary's eye. "In the mansion," he mouthed.

Motioning to the guys, Mark placed the thick cloth back into Guenther's mouth. With the help of Jack, they lifted him off the stiff chair and dragged him into the guest bedroom at the back of the house. The men threw the furious and wiggling Guenther on the bed. Once Mark made sure the windows were locked and the blinds drawn, Guenther was left alone.

When they returned to the living room, Mark said, "I think we need a moment to talk."

"Thanks, yes," said a teary Gary. "I want to know what you guys think."

"Are you all right?" said Jack, leaning forward.

"Yeah, I'm fine. At least we know Anne's still alive, but for how long?" said Gary whose face showed lines of worry.

"We can't allow Guenther to return to the mansion," said Jack.

"Yes, I agree," said Mike. He smiled. "What do you have in mind?"

"This seems the safest place for now. We can take turns watching him until we take Harold down. Then we can free him," said Jack. He rested against the back of his chair and folded his arms.

"How do we recover Anne?" asked Ted, throwing his arms in the air. "That should be our top priority."

"If we could get Guenther to tell us where in the mansion she is being held, then it might be easier to free her," said Gary. He was so worried that his body shook.

"I don't think he's going to be forthcoming with that information," said Mike.

"We'll just have to torture him a bit. We could enter the Hartley mansion and get her out. Thanks to the film Anne taped, we have the complete layout," said Gary, thinking faster than he could speak.

"That's obviously very helpful," said Peter. "But how do we get in?"

Jack laughed. "I have the perfect way in. Through the Walgreens truck. We could hide in it and could get into the mansion without anyone noticing."

"What about all the surveillance cameras?" asked Ted.

The men sat in deep thought until Mike said, "We could cut the electricity. That would blind the cameras."

The men nodded.

"That would work," said Mark.

"I think you should leave the rescuing to us policemen," said Mike. "They wouldn't harm a policeman."

"Let me go and get the location out of him," said Gary ready to inflict some pain on Guenther as revenge for Anne's incarceration.

"No," said Mike. "I'll do that. I know how to break him. He's just the follower of an insane man. I'll find a way into his mind."

Peter stood up. "Gary, you need to get out of here. Why don't you and Ted go to that Indian restaurant we passed on our way here and get us something for dinner? We're going to be here a while."

"Okay," Gary said reluctantly.

Ted grabbed the van's keys off the side table and happily linked arms with Gary to haul him to his feet. Gary really didn't want to go anywhere but the guys were right. He had to get some fresh air.

After Ted and Gary had left the house, Mike telephoned Allan and Chuck and told them to join them in Maggie's house. They said they'll be right over.

As soon as he hung up the phone, Mike gestured to Mark, and they rose from their chairs and made their way into the back bedroom to interrogate Guenther.

Jack and Peter remained in the living room. All was silent for a few minutes, then they heard Guenther scream. It was more of an angry scream than a painful scream. Neither man wanted to know what Mike was doing so they jumped up to scope out Maggie's kitchen. They retrieved plates and cutlery. Jack found some napkins, and they spread everything out over the dining room table.

By the time Jack and Peter had returned to the living room, Gary and Ted arrived with the food. They were excited with what they had found. They bought dishes of samosa, pakoras, garlic naan, shrimp madas, beef vindaloo and chicken masala, which all looked great.

Mike and Mark soon joined the others and they all sat down to enjoy this delicious meal and discuss Guenther's interrogation.

"So what have you got?" said Gary ready to burst.

"We've got him where we want him. He needs to sit and think about his situation now. Hopefully, when we bring him some food, he'll give in and tell us where Anne is being held," said Mike. Using the spoons provided, he dished out the food onto his plate.

"He's doing a great job," said Mark, enjoying the spicy food. "Mike has Guenther wondering what's going on."

"Gary, where's the disc with the video footage?" asked Jack. He put down his cutlery and prepared to get up.

"I'll get it." Gary rose from the dining table and strolled into the living room where he had left his belongings.

Opening his brown leather briefcase, Gary retrieved the expected disc. He grabbed his laptop and turned it on. Then he inserted the disc, which opened up into Anne's view of the mansion. He carried his laptop to the dining room and placed it on the table in such a way that everyone could see what was being shown on the screen.

Gary started the program and the men viewed the video in silence. Rising in front of them were images from inside the Hartley mansion. The men were astonished by the stunning bleakness of the place, the plain halls and rooms, the grey kitchen, the open vestibule, and organized computer room.

Suddenly, a loud knock sounded on the front door, and everyone jumped in their seats. Peter was the first to rise and answered the door with Mike one step behind him. Two policemen stood on the stoop. Mike introduced Allan and Chuck to the poker buddies.

Once everyone was acquainted, the policemen explained their efforts to recover Anne and were shown Anne's film footage. It was agreed that they should attempt to infiltrate the Hartley mansion to recover her. Now that they knew the layout, the idea of successfully entering the house was clear and simple. Through Jack's previous success, they decided to enter the grounds using the Walgreens delivery truck.

It made its delivery every Wednesday. Allan and Chuck accepted their assigned roles and agreed to ride in the back of the van. Mike would take over as driver.

"I have a few injections of that sedative we used for the Walgreens driver," said Peter. "I brought them along just in case we had to sedate Guenther."

"That's great," said Mike. Mike handed the video over to Allan and Chuck to memorize. Once their plans were fixed, the policemen left Maggie's house. Mike and Mark marched into the guest bedroom to continue with their endeavors with Guenther.

The remaining poker buddies cleaned up the dining room and washed all the dishes. They then returned to the living room to await the verdict from the silent back bedroom.

They waited hours. The moon had risen and stars shone bright. Since they were exhausted, they decided to get some sleep. Mark would wake them when they had news.

Jack and Ted took Maggie's bed and Peter and Gary accepted the couches in the living room. They grabbed some pillows from a closet as well as blankets folded in a pile on a shelf.

As morning broke, Mike and Mark were finally successful. They woke up the guys and they gathered in the living room.

"We have it," said Mike. "After a long night of Mike's hard work, Guenther folded like a broke poker player. We now know where Anne is being held and thanks to the video, we'll have no problems infiltrating that part of the mansion."

"That's great," said Gary, feeling so relieved.

"Why don't the rest of you return to Jack's cottage? I think it would look suspicious for all of us to be here together," said Mark.

"He's right," said Mike. "Why don't you leave now? I'll drive you to the airport. We'll find Anne."

"We could stay at a hotel?" said Ted.

"No. It's dangerous for you to remain," said Mike.

"Fine," said Jack. "We'll leave but if anything, and I mean anything, comes up, tell us, and we will be on the next flight."

"Don't worry guys. I'll keep you informed. Something's got to give. Go home and take care of your families," said Mark.

"I'm staying," said Gary. He got no argument from his friends.

Ted, Jack, and Peter gathered their belongings, and Mike drove them to the airport. Once he had let them off, Mike was relieved. It was just too risky for them to be seen together.

Back at Maggie's house, Mark and Gary discussed how best to watch Guenther and keep him from escaping. Mark constantly had to restrain Gary from going into the guest bedroom and hurting Guenther. Gary was so angry about Anne's captivity that he wanted to hang him.

Mark sent Gary on a mission to find a hardware store and buy an appropriate lock for the bedroom door and one for each of the windows in the bedroom. Guenther was still tied up on the bed, and they couldn't leave him like that all night. While Gary was out shopping, Mark decided to sit with Guenther to see if he could find out any more about Harold.

Reaching the back bedroom, Mark put his ear against the door but heard nothing. When he opened the door, he found Guenther stretched out and motionless.

Mark stomped over to the bed and shook Guenther into consciousness.

"Who is that? Who are you?" asked Guenther in a groggy voice.

"My name is Mark. Would you like to share some more?"

"With you? Where's the other guy?"

Mike had been the only one to speak to Guenther so far. Mark had stayed at his side during the whole interrogation but only in the capacity of secretary to record everything Guenther said. Since he had time now, he thought he'd try to get him to divulge more.

"He's left. It's just you and me. Is there anything you would like to get off your chest?"

"If Harold discovers I've been kidnapped, he'll destroy you," Guenther said, trying to sound as confident as possible.

Calling his bluff, Mark said, "No one knows you're here. And your stay will be of some duration unless you answer our questions."

"You can't use me against Harold. I won't hurt his chances to control the world." Guenther wrestled with the handcuffs around his wrists.

"You really think that's possible?" Mark's mouth dropped.

"Look around. Everyone's afraid of their own shadows. We control the people." He tried to remove the blindfold with his shoulders.

"We? So that does include you?" Mark crossed his arms across his chest.

"Of course it includes me." Guenther laughed.

"What position will you have?"

Guenther pursed his lips.

Mark said, "Harold is just carrying you around as his slave. You have a chance to save yourself if you talk to me. Harold will be taken down and sent to jail as a traitor. Do you want the same thing to happen to you?"

"You can't take down Harold. I'm not afraid of you," said Guenther as he squirmed on the bed.

"We'll take him down. I can assure you of that. We have the police, people in the media and the government assisting us. Soon, we'll know everything and Harold will end up in jail."

Mark could feel Guenther's emotions going up and down. One minute he felt powerful, and then the next minute, his defiant attitude crashed. Mark was getting to him and hoped he would soon divulge every detail.

Mark decided to try a different tack.

"How long have you been following Harold?" Mark put out a hand to stop Guenther from moving.

"Years." Guenther jumped back at the touch.

"Where did you meet?"

"Does it matter? Why are you asking me these things?" Guenther rolled from side to side.

"I'm curious. Where did you meet Harold?" Mark stood beside the bed and looked down at Guenther.

"At a university in Germany. Harold had a sabbatical there in the late 90s. I was a pupil." Guenther shrugged his shoulders as if to say he didn't think this information was of any consequence.

Mark wrote this down then said, "So you're not the one killing people?"

"I'm not telling you that." Guenther leaned back until he was lying straight.

"Why not? We won't allow you to return to the mansion. You might as well tell me everything because it will only help your cause. We have the power now." Mark grabbed Guenther and pulled him into a seated position.

Guenther tried to escape Mark's grasp and spat, "You really think so? You have no idea what you are up against."

"And what are we up against?" he asked holding him erect.

Guenther paused. He turned his face to Mark's even though he couldn't see him through the blindfold. He said, "The most lethal group of men."

"Does Harold command them?" He pushed him back.

"Yes, of course. Harold is in control of everything." He tried again to release himself from Mark's grasp.

But Mark wouldn't let him go. "So if we stop Harold, we stop the whole system, right?"

"You can't beat Harold. He'll win every time." He wrenched himself free.

Just as Mark was about to ask him another question, he heard the front door slam shut. Gary had returned with the locks. Without saying a word, Gary entered the guest bedroom. He passed Mark a screwdriver then attached a lock to the bedroom door. Mark set about fixing the lock for the only window.

The men worked quickly and efficiently and completed their work in no time. Once the locks were adjusted and checked, Gary left the room. Mark put on a ski mask. He then unlocked Guenther's bound hands and removed the blindfold covering his eyes.

As if he had been stung by bees, Guenther rubbed and scratched his itchy face then drew his fingers through his messy hair.

"You're all dead men. Dead I tell you. Once Harold discovers I'm missing, he'll send out the worst people you can ever imagine to find me. Then he'll destroy you."

Mark laughed then closed the bedroom door and locked it from the outside. Mark wasn't quite sure what they were going to do with him, but it was obvious that they could not free him. He did consider the fact that the longer they held him, the more information he would give to them. Of course, Guenther would be treated well. They weren't violent men.

From the living room door, Mark watched Gary make up the couch into a bed, leaving Maggie's bedroom for him. Mark found a couple of pillows for Gary and wished him goodnight. Both men were very tired. It had been a long day.

As soon as Guenther had been left alone in the bedroom, he quickly leapt off the bed and completely searched the small bedroom. The new lock on the sturdy door was steadfast and would not budge. He desperately tried the window but it was solidly locked shut.

Guenther opened and closed every drawer and shelf in the bedroom, searching for anything that would give him information about where he was or a means to escape, but he came up empty. He had no choice but disrobe and get into the clean white sheets of the comfortable single bed.

However, Guenther couldn't sleep. Over and over in his cluttered mind, he constantly played out the abduction. He wondered how he could have evaded these men. What could he have done to escape? Only then did Guenther realize he was stuck and there was no way out of his capture. He would try to remain strong and resist but deep down, he was afraid to give in. If his captors were to press the right buttons, he could break.

The last thought on Guenther's tired mind as he fell into a restless sleep was what Harold would do when he realized that he had disappeared.

WEDNESDAY AFTERNOON

The three policemen dressed in the Walgreens uniform waited as the Walgreens delivery truck driver exited the convenience store's back door. As the driver settled into his seat, Chuck injected the unsuspecting driver with Peter's wonderful potion, then caught him when he fell unconscious. Allan and Mike dashed forward and gently placed the man in the back of his delivery truck. Mike took over as the Walgreens driver. Allan and Chuck jumped into the back of the truck.

Mike pulled the truck out into traffic and headed for 320 Sycamore Avenue, Bethesda. On the seat beside him were Tony's clear directions. They arrived at their destination without incident. Mike pulled into the Hartley driveway and stopped at the metal gates. Immediately, the huge gate swung open.

Mike slowly drove up the white gravel road into the rear parking lot. He positioned the truck in such a way that the vehicle's rear was closest to the back door, where two older men, dressed in black aprons, waited.

One chef came forward when Mike jumped out of the truck.

"Who are you? Where's Scott?" demanded the chef.

"Sick. Taking his route today," said Mike.

"He seems to be sick a lot lately. Do you have identification?"

Mike handed over the fake Walgreens employee card along with a similarly phony driver's license. The chefs scrutinized these documents and then grunted.

"Proceed," said the older chef, handing Mike back his fake documents.

Allan and Chuck had piled the expected boxes against the back door. When Mike opened these doors, the two policeman hid in the back of the truck. Mike then placed the boxes on a trolley and pushed it into the house.

One of the two waiting chefs held the door open for him, and then both men followed Mike into the busy kitchen. With the coast clear, Allan and Chuck jumped out of the truck and made their way into the huge kitchen hoping to remain invisible.

While the chefs and their assistants were busy putting away the boxes, Allan and Chuck passed completely unnoticed through the kitchen and into the open and airy vestibule. They made their way over to a small door which lead to the house's fuse box.

After pulling then extracting a fuse lever, the house fell into darkness. They turned on their flashlights then slipped across the area and into the maintenance room following Gary's written directions. Listening at the door, they could hear people talking excitedly probably trying to discover the reason for the lack of electricity, but no one was in sight.

Sliding along the wall, Allan and Chuck rushed into a back stairwell that led them to the fourth floor attic in the east wing. On their toes, they silently jumped up the stairs. When they reached the attic, they peered into the hallway. Hearing a sound, they held themselves against the wall.

A maid left one of the rooms and made her way slowly to the main stairwell. When her steps could no longer be heard, the men slipped into the hallway. They tried each door, but they were locked tight.

Chuck put his ear up to the doors. Picking out one, he expertly opened the lock but the room was empty. He tried the next door. That room was also empty. Allan pointed out the last room, and Chuck tried that lock. He opened the door to find a young woman lying in the fetal position on the bed, the only piece of furniture in the room.

"Anne Martin?" Allan asked.

The frightened, brown-haired lady still dressed in her Harvey Girls uniform nodded and began to shake.

"Relax. We're police officers, and we're here to rescue you," said Chuck.

Anne burst into tears and ran into their arms.

"We'll get you out of here. Follow us," Allan said as Chuck checked the dark hallway.

The area was empty and the surveillance cameras were turned off. The policemen and Anne quickly snuck out of the attic and down the back stairwell. They used their flashlights to retrace their steps. When they reached the east wing, they could hear people moving about. Chuck held Anne, and they crouched on the bottom steps, hoping no one came that way.

Using her hands, Anne explained a short cut through the east wing and back out to the main vestibule. Running as quickly and as quietly as possible, they made their way to the vestibule. Allan snuck a look and noticed people moving about in the dark. Anne ducked into a small room, and the men followed. Chuck stayed by the door and kept it open a crack so he could evaluate the situation.

After a few nervous moments, doors were closed, and the vestibule emptied. Anne and the cops ran across the room and slipped into the maintenance closet. Breathing a little heavily, they stayed there for a few moments. Not hearing a sound, they snuck out and ran into the kitchen.

Once there, they realized Mike was keeping the Hartley staff busy by pretending to argue about their invoice. He held a paper before them so their backs were turned away from the door. When Allan stuck his nose in, Mike encouraged them forward. Allan, Chuck, and Anne carefully slipped through the huge kitchen and made it easily out the back door. Chuck threw the necessary fuse into the bushes and then they jumped into the back of the Walgreens van.

Once he knew they were safe, Mike made a quick exit from the Hartley mansion. He threw the trolley into the truck. Smiling at their success, he closed the back door. With as much speed as possible without drawing attention to himself, Mike drove the delivery truck back to the Walgreens main parking lot. When it was placed in the same position as the other Walgreens trucks,

Mike put the truck into park and ran out to open the heavy back doors.

Allan and Chuck held the Walgreens driver in their arms and placed him back into the driver's seat. They arranged him in a seated position so when the man woke up, he would think he had gone to sleep at the wheel. Once the front seat was organized, the police officers and Anne walked a block to a public parking lot, where Allan had left his police vehicle.

As soon as everyone was seated safely in the police car, Allan pulled out into traffic.

Finally, Anne found her voice and asked, "How did you find me?"

"Thanks to your excellent video of the mansion and a bit of persuasion from Guenther," said Chuck who sat beside Anne in the back seat.

"Where's Gary?" Anne body's still shook.

"At Maggie's house. We're headed there now," said Mike.

"How were you treated?" asked Chuck.

"Okay. I wasn't hurt only kept in seclusion. I saw no one but a maid who delivered my meals."

"You didn't see anyone else?" Mike asked.

"No. When I was discovered, I was taken into a room we never entered. Only the main housekeeper cleaned that room. It was empty except for Guenther."

"Go on. We want to know everything," said Allan.

Anne breathed deeply a few times as if she was finally allowed to breathe again. It felt good being safe. She'd had no idea what they were going to do to her.

"Guenther demanded to know for whom I was working and why I interfered with their computers. I kept telling him that I didn't know what he was talking about, but he became angry with me." Remembering the situation, her body stiffened, and she closed her eyes.

"I'm sorry," said Chuck.

"You're a strong woman," said Mike. "You must have been scared."

"Yes, I was. For several hours, Guenther continued to try to get me to talk. He told me that he had people to do the dirty work. If I didn't answer his questions, he would have me killed. After the interview, I was locked away in that attic room."

"Did you meet Harold?" asked Mike.

"No," said Anne. "I never saw him, but Ian visited me and attempted to interrogate me."

"How did that go?" asked Chuck.

"He didn't get anything from me."

By this time, Allan had turned the car into Maggie's neighbourhood and right up to her townhouse. When Mark and Gary heard the car pulling into the driveway, they ran outside. Anne fell into Gary's waiting arms. They cried in happiness and relief.

The men shook hands and patted each other's back congratulating themselves on the success of their mission. They were exhausted and glad to be back on safe ground. Finally able to relax, they burst out laughing as a release from the stress.

Gary and Anne hugged each other tightly. They looked into each other's eyes and kissed feverishly.

"I love you so much," said Gary.

"I know, sweetheart. I love you too," said Anne.

Gary kept apologizing over and over again. "I'm so sorry to put you in such a dangerous situation." He kissed and held her as if to prove she was real.

"It had to be done," said Anne, smiling sadly.

"I feel so bad," said Gary. "I'm so relieved you weren't hurt."

"No, they didn't hurt me. I'm fine."

"I can't believe I have you back."

"I'm back and I'm not leaving your side ever again." Anne laughed with relief.

Glancing around the neighbourhood, Mark pushed them into Maggie's house. They hadn't been seen but didn't want to take any chances. The policemen followed Mark into the house. Anne and Gary soon joined them and everyone fell into the living room. The men took the chairs and sofas, leaving the loveseat for Anne and Gary, who couldn't take their eyes or hands off each other.

"You should return immediately to Boston," said Chuck.

"The sooner you get out of D.C., the better," said Allan.

"I'll drive you to the airport," said Mike.

It was decided that Mark would remain at Maggie's house to further interrogate Guenther. He would keep his friends at the cottage informed. It was decided that only Mark and Mike should handle Guenther. Hopefully, with the right pressure, they would learn the truth from him, and he would give them enough information to destroy Harold.

WEDNESDAY EVENING

A sudden, loud knock sounded on the heavy wooden door of Harold's private study. Since Ian wasn't there, Harold just sat in his chair and waited. After a few moments, the heavy door opened to reveal Franz, wearing a dark blue golf shirt tucked into black jeans.

Franz walked directly over to Harold's chair and stood in silence.

"Did you find him?" Harold said.

"No. We've searched the whole mansion."

"Who saw him last?"

"Richard, the chauffeur. On Monday, Guenther left in his car to retrieve the mail. Richard never saw him return."

"Find him!"

Franz bowed his head then briskly exited his study.

Franz marched down the short hallway and into the large office he shared with Guenther. It was a splendid room big enough to hold four people but only housed the two. Since they had been working together for a while now, the cousins had become completely in tune with each other's personalities. Franz had no explanation for Guenther's disappearance.

Grabbing his car keys off his desk, Franz made his way out of the office. At the far end of the hallway, he unlocked a thick steel door leading to a narrow, metal stairwell reaching into the   depths of the Hartley mansion.

Walking down some steps, Franz entered a silent stone cavern. He followed the secret tunnel for ten minutes when he reached another metal stairwell. He climbed to another steel door leading to a large elevator requiring a special key.

Franz waited for the elevator to reach him and take him to the main level of a tall, glass office building. Franz marched to the far end of the parking lot reserved for Harold's employees' vehicles. Only a select few knew of this exit. This way they could come and go from the Hartley mansion without being seen. He jumped into his black Ford pick-up.

When he reached G and Pennsylvania streets, he recognized Guenther's silver SUV parked outside the post office. A tow truck had harnessed the vehicle and was preparing to tow it away.

Franz parked behind the tow truck. He leapt out of his car and ran up to the tow truck driver.

"What are you doing?" asked Franz.

"This vehicle has been abandoned. I'm towing it to the lot," said the tow truck vehicle.

"I know the owner of this car."

"Do you have any documentation to prove that?"

"No, but I will remove it myself."

"Too late, buddy. It's going to the lot. Here's a receipt with its location. You can pick it up there."

With no recourse, Franz accepted the slip of paper. He quickly looked over Guenther's car for any evidence to explain Guenther's disappearance, but there was none. He was terrified of Harold's retribution if he should return to the mansion without Guenther.

* * *

The sound of a vehicle driving up the private road caused the inhabitants of Jack's cottage to drop everything and run outside to see who was arriving. They were thrilled to see Gary but were ecstatic when they spied Anne in the seat beside him. They barely allowed Gary to park the car before the relieved group fell upon the happy couple.

Upon seeing her mother, Renee began to cry. She had been very strong during this whole ordeal and never gave up believing that her mother was alive, but now her emotions got the better of her.

"How did you escape?" asked Susan when Renee's happiness had died down.

"Mike and his two cop friends rescued me. It's quite a story. I can't wait to tell you."

"Eat first," said Ruth. "We have plenty of time to hear your story."

The whole group swarmed into the warm kitchen where they retrieved food from the fridge. After Anne and Gary were pushed into chairs at the dining table, a delicious assortment of roast chicken, vegetables, and salad was placed before them.

"Eat!" Ruth ordered.

Anne and Gary happily feasted. The rest of the group left them alone and drifted into the living room where they waited for Anne and Gary to join them.

As soon as the happy couple strolled into the room, Maggie asked, "Where's Mark?"

"Back at your house. We have Guenther locked in your guest bedroom. Mark and Mike are attempting to squeeze more information out of him," said Gary.

Ruth's mouth dropped. "He's still our prisoner?"

"Yes. We might be able to get more out of him," said Gary, helping Anne onto the couch. She was a little stiff.

"Maybe keeping him is a good idea," said Ted. "We can't have him returning to Harold and exposing us."

"I just hope that won't put them in any danger," said Ruth.

"Don't worry," said Gary. "They won't be discovered."

"What's our next move?" asked Peter. He leaned back in his chair and crossed his legs.

"Let's wait and see what Mark can get," said Gary, tightly holding Anne's hand.

The group dispersed to take care of their children. After the kids were settled in bed, the adults came together in the living room to hear Anne's tale. She was finally able to relax after her dangerous ordeal.

Once everyone was seated comfortably, Anne began. "After we had completed our work on

Wednesday, Flo, who is Harold's main housekeeper, confronted me. She led me into Harold's study."

"Did she know who you were?" asked Susan.

"She said nothing to me."

"Did you meet Harold?" asked Jack.

"No. The only person in the study was Guenther. He knew that I had set up a flash drive on their computers. He told me that I would be remaining in that house until they found out the damage I had done. At first, I wouldn't tell him anything, but he threatened me until I gave up the USB stick."

"So he knows you have seen everything?" asked Ted.

A deep sigh rose from the group realizing how close Anne had come to danger.

"After a couple of hours, Guenther gave up. I was blindfolded then taken to a room in the attic. I was kept in seclusion and only saw a young woman who delivered the meals."

"Poor Anne," said Ruth. "I'm so sorry you had to endure that."

"Yes, poor Anne," said Laura. "We didn't realize the danger we'd be putting you in."

"I'm sorry too. Anything we can do for you?" asked Peter.

"I'm fine," said Anne. "I've got everything I need." She hugged her husband and looked around the room smiling at everyone.

"How did they treat you?" asked Ted.

"I ate well and wasn't harmed, but I was kept in silence. That was torture enough."

"So sorry, my love," said Gary.

"It's okay. It's not your fault. It was my choice to do this," said Anne.

"Can you talk about your escape?" asked Jack.

"Sure," said Anne. "Yesterday afternoon, two police men broke into my room. I was amazed to see them. We made it out of the mansion unseen. The rescue was so quick I hardly had time to breathe."

"Wonderful guys," said Gary.

"As soon as I saw Gary at Maggie's, I knew I was safe. We owe those men a huge debt of gratitude."

"We sure do," said Gary. "They also helped us get out of the city and back here."

"I'm so glad to be back," said Anne. "Thank you for taking care of Renee."

"We're a family," said Laura.

"We'll always be there for each other," said Jack.

Everyone smiled at each other. It was a relaxed and happy atmosphere.

Becoming serious again, Ted said, "So, apart from waiting for the cops, what do we do now?"

"It's about time Gary revive his radio show," said Jack.

"Are you kidding? Where from? Here?" said Gary.

"Yes, here," said Jack.

"Why?" asked Ted. "What's rolling around in that brain of yours?"

"What if we contact people directly and encourage them to join us against Harold?" said Jack.

"And then we'll know where we stand," said Ted finishing off Jack's thought.

"Won't somebody be able to trace us?" Susan asked.

"Not if we do it through an anonymous website account," said Jack.

"That's not a bad idea," said Peter. "We could be the voice of rebellion."

"We hold all the cards," said Jack.

"Yes, and together, we could write the shows," said Gary.

The poker buddies and their wives stared at each other as if debating this notion. Ideas about what they could say were rolling around in their minds. Everyone was excited. They had to expose Harold, share what they knew, and encourage people to rebel against Harold. The radio show would present the perfect format.

"What should we name the site?" said Peter.

"How about Harold's Little Rebels?" smiled Ruth.

Everyone burst into laughter as they considered her idea. It felt good to laugh.

"What about the New Society?" said Laura, grabbing some paper from the desk.

"Or Follow Us," said Susan, holding out a pen.

"I like Save Yourselves," said Ted.

Peter held up his hand and said, "What about Harold's Enemies?"

"No, I don't think so," said Jack. "I like follow us. That's to the point and direct. I'll register the site and set it up. The rest of you decide what Gary should say."

"Shouldn't it deal with what life would be like without Harold?" said Ruth.

"Yes," said Gary. "We could start there. Americans should know they have a choice."

"Let them know someone opposes Harold," said Peter, standing up.

"That should get people talking," said Gary. He pulled out his laptop.

"The first thing we should do is make sure the people are safe and not worried about being discovered. What would you say to posing the question: Are you a particle at rest?" said Ted.

"Yes, that's good. The uncertainty principle," said Gary.

Peter rhymed off the definition for their wives, "The principle that the momentum and position of a particle cannot both be precisely determined at the same time."

Ted moved over to sit beside Gary on the couch and said, "By saying we are a particle at rest, people will understand that we're in hiding and safe from Harold's influence."

"That would work," said Peter.

The group discussed material Gary could pose in his radio show.

"It's essential we create a scenario with which everyone can identify," said Laura.

"I agree," said Ted. "We must reach out to the American public and convince them to oppose Harold."

"We should show them a life without Harold," said Peter.

"Could anyone find us?" asked Susan, a little terrified about where this might lead.

"No," said Gary. "I'll put up so many fire walls, no one will be able to trace the show."

"Are you sure?" asked Ruth also worried for their lives.

"Sure," said Gary.

"I'll create a website and set up a video for live streaming," said Jack. "I'll write a short opening advising that Gary's radio show will resume at ten a.m. tomorrow."

Ted encouraged everyone to get on their computers and tweet the scheduled meeting to all of their followers.

"I heard from McAlister today. Remember the newspaper guy?" After everyone nodded, Gary continued, "His article is ready and will be published in tomorrow's paper. I'll ask him to include the radio show."

The whole group went to bed excited about what tomorrow would bring. Gary's speech was written and they all agreed it was good and should influence the American public. They hoped they could break Harold's influence.

THURSDAY

After breakfast, Gary and Jack moved into the study and sat down at the computer to prepare for Gary's radio show. While Gary set up a microphone and webcam, Jack transferred some of Gary's promotional pictures and recognizable slogans to the colorful site.

Allowing Gary and Jack some solitude, the poker buddies, women, and children prepared to listen to Gary's radio show on Peter's laptop in the living room. Everyone was nervous. They had all been working long and hard on Gary's speech and wondered how it would go over with the American public.   Peter called Mark at Maggie's house to advise him about the show. He would listen to it with Mike. Mark had received some positive news from the two detectives, who would arrive at Maggie's house in the early afternoon. He promised to contact Gary as soon as he could and wished him good luck.

At precisely ten a.m., Gary began a live-streaming video from his website. They set up the podcast so there could be interaction between Gary and his audience. Anyone listening in could express their opinions without any fear of exposure.

He introduced himself in his usual manner hopefully putting people at ease. "Welcome to *Science Today*. I'm Gary Martin coming to you via the Internet instead of my usual home at KPH radio station. We'll begin our show with the question: Are you a particle at rest?"

Silence. Gary and Jack looked at the attendance box in the corner. It showed the number of hits on the site. More than a thousand people were listening but no sound came from the computer.

"Are you avoiding the uncertainty principle?" asked Gary and paused waiting to see if there would be a response. "That of not being able to trace?"

Suddenly, the hits greatly increased by the thousands. Jack and Gary smiled as they saw the number grow. Soon a million were listening. Pleased with the attention, Gary nodded to his friend and continued.

"I'm a particle at rest," said Gary. "Are you?"

A few seconds later, a voice piped in, "To avoid violating the uncertainty principle, you're completely ignorant of its position. You could be anywhere."

"Exactly," said Gary. "How about you, my friend?"

"I'm also a particle at rest," said the voice who introduced himself as Jeff.

"Can we join in too?" interrupted another male voice. "I'm Herman and my wife Jenny is here with me. We're also particles at rest."

"I'm another particle at rest," said a man who introduced himself as Tom.

More voices flooded in from the site until there was a feeling of a town hall meeting. Many people declared themselves safe and free to talk. It was more than the poker buddies had dare hoped. Obviously, there were many unhappy people out there who wanted a change from Harold. They were all willing to disobey him and take matters into their own hands. Their number swelled to millions. Everyone must have stayed home from work to listen.

"Okay, everyone," Gary said after the loud noise had become too great to distinguish anyone's individual voice.

Once the voices died down, a nervous female voice eked out, "Are you still sending in the reports?"

"No," said Gary.

"Neither am I," said another male voice.

"Same here," said two more males.

All the voices assented. Everyone admitted to no longer sending reports to Harold. Numerous people divulged that they had moved someplace safe. They were not afraid of Harold coming after them, and so everyone was finally speaking openly about their precarious situation.

"Be very careful," warned Gary. "We're all in danger. You must be aware of everything. Harold has some sort of hit squad. They seem invisible, but people go missing."

"Invisible is right," said a female voice. "Everyone should look out for any suspicious characters. We could share our findings here."

Sounds of approval came from the consensus of people monitoring the website. The longer the program continued, the more people announced their presence. The poker buddies were agog to see the total hits passing the ten million mark. It was an unmanageable response, but they were pleased to finally have an army to fight Harold.

"Has anyone seen or met Harold?" said a male voice.

There was chorus of "no."

As yet, the poker buddies were not prepared to admit that they had kidnapped Guenther. There was time enough for everything, and they could not be positively sure everyone online could be trusted.

"Does anyone know where he can be found?" asked a squeaky feminine voice.

Another chorus of "no" rang out from the computer. This was one of the secrets the men had agreed to divulge because they wanted people to believe that Harold was going down.

As soon as a pause occurred, Gary said, "I've discovered his home. I won't give out that address until we have a purpose. When the time is right, we'll descend upon him."

"Tell me where the bastard lives," said one angry male. "I'll go there now and bash his head in."

Many agreed.

"What's Harold's address? I'll go there and kill him," said the voices.

But Harold was smart, and the poker buddies knew that they had to plan something airtight before they committed a frontal attack. They explained this to their listeners, hoping to calm them down.

＊ ＊ ＊

Franz made his way to Harold's study. Harold had been holed up in there all morning, preparing for the next step in controlling the United States. He wrote a series of speeches to be given at rallies organized by Guenther. He would travel the U.S. and convince Americans that he was the right man to take over the country. He would become invincible and the total submission of the American people would be complete.

Knocking at Harold's study door, Franz waited for a response. He continued to wait for at least ten minutes until he finally decided to enter the room. He worried about Harold's response to his intrusion because he had been so furious earlier. So many people had stopped sending in their reports.

He found Harold concentrating over a pile of papers on his huge desk. Harold made no indication that he was in the room until Franz stood near his chair and cleared his throat.

"What is it?" Harold grunted.

"Guenther's disappeared."

"What has been done to locate him?"

"His car was impounded. He was last seen at the post office. From there, his trail is cold."

"Find him."

"And then?"

"Kill him," growled Harold.

Immediately, Franz turned on his heel and left the room. He opened Harold's study door and spied Flo standing in the hallway with a look of terror on her face.

"What's the matter?" asked Franz.

"That woman is gone," Flo said. Her body shaking.

"What?" Franz responded with shock.

"The maid just returned. She's gone."

"She must be somewhere in the house. Gather everyone. Begin a rigorous search pattern. She has to be here."

Franz entered the war room and organized the employees into pairs to search the Hartley mansion. It was unbelievable that their prisoner had escaped. They were sure Anne was safely imprisoned.

Entering his office, Franz slumped into his chair and turned on his computer. He checked to make sure the surveillance cameras were in good working order and then reviewed the video to see if she showed up on any of them.

Then the cameras went black and Franz remembered that the electricity had died for a couple of hours. A fuse had gone missing from the fuse box. When a replacement had been found, the electricity came on without any difficulty. Franz figured that's when she escaped.

Every nook and cranny of the massive mansion was searched. When all the employees had returned, it was obvious that she had disappeared.

The mansion had been infiltrated and Franz wondered if Guenther's disappearance had anything to do with Anne's extrication. He couldn't believe that Guenther had freed Anne, and they had escaped together. He didn't want to be the one to inform Harold of this latest disaster, but he had no choice.

One solid knock sounded at Harold's study door. Franz waited a number of minutes until he overcame his nervousness and opened the door. Harold was still sitting over his desk and was furious at being disturbed again.

Without raising his head, Harold shouted, "What do you want now?"

"That woman is gone," said Franz.

"Gone? How?"

"She's nowhere to be found. We've searched the entire mansion. No one saw anything."

"Your incompetence disgusts me."

"I'll look for her immediately."

"I don't want to see you again until Guenther and that woman are found."

Backing out of his study, Franz left Harold, knowing that his days were numbered if he didn't locate Guenther and Anne. He worried and wondered if Harold's plans were in jeopardy. Everything was falling apart.

* * *

When the radio show reached the two-hour mark, Gary cleared his throat and said, "Everyone. Please quiet down. I have some words that need to be spoken."

After the millions of voices died down, Gary began his speech. "I want to discuss life and its meaning. We must live a better life away from struggles. Harold's world is not for us, and we must break free.

"Knowing poker can greatly assist in understanding how best to live your life. Life and poker have many similarities. Let me explain how those similarities will make you able to live in a world without Harold.

"Life can deal you a good hand or a bad one. In Harold's world, only bad hands appear. Without Harold, good hands are possible. No matter which you receive, you should attempt to achieve the best possible results. Though there is no choice on the kind of hand you receive, it's what you do with that hand which can change your life for the better.

"With every hand, you should be striving for the nuts: the best winning hand. The perfect hand. That winning hand guarantees you to move forward whether it be in a game of poker or in life. By reaching for your goals, you are also achieving that perfect winning situation.

"In Harold's world, you have no chance to win with any hand. Your cards are held back.

"If you're free from Harold, a chance for a winning hand is possible. You'll feel a rush of adrenalin giving you energy and excitement greatly improving your life.

It's a rush being successful at something. Honesty and hard work are paramount, but not in Harold's deceitful, lying world where no one has a chance to succeed.

"No more Harold means that you'll be able to make a bet putting you out there in the world. Whether it be for employment, to make friends, to travel to a new place, or anything else which betters your world. As you bet on a poker hand, you must bet on opportunities in life, hoping to improve your situation in life. If you don't bet, you can't win. Therefore, take every possible opportunity and chance provided to you. Harold offers no opportunity for you to bet on anything in life.

"In life and poker, there is failure. It hurts when you lose a hand, but if you keep playing, you'll get over that hurt and continue on. Many losses occur in life. It's how you get up, brush yourself off, and move on that matters. There is only loss in Harold's world. It's not a tragedy to lose, but it is if you give up. No one should give up. We can rid ourselves of Harold.

"To get ahead in life, sometimes you have to bluff, an opportunity not allowed in Harold's world. You can't always determine what is a bluff unless you watch someone closely and see how they play their other hands. You must bluff with some things in life to be successful. This doesn't mean lying, which is a different ballgame altogether. A bluff is an honest risk-taking adventure where you can outplay any opponents. Nothing is wrong with taking a chance now and then because these risks can only improve your life and your position at the poker table.

"Another opportunity not allowed in Harold's world is to go all-in. You throw all your money or chips into the center of the table hoping to win the greatest amount. You have to believe you possess the best possible hand at the table and that you are willing to gamble with it. Succeeding this way is exciting and invigorating, helping you achieve great things.

"To go all-in or not to go all-in, that is the question. You put forth all your effort, knowledge, and abilities towards a new job, a new relationship, or anything else in your life. With every step in life and in a poker game, you must take it full of empowerment and excitement. Only by putting everything into your dreams, will you succeed. To achieve anything in life requires an all-in effort, which isn't allowed in Harold's world.

"There is such a thing as being on tilt in a poker game. That's when you are unable to win any hand. Just bad luck. Everyone goes through a bad stretch. Having Harold controlling us has put us on a bad streak. The important thing is not to become depressed and give up. We can beat Harold by staying confident and keep playing. You don't know when you will break out of that bad streak and start winning again. We can beat Harold and rid ourselves of that bad streak. Don't let it get you down.

"Succeeding in poker and in life are very similar. Both involve luck and skill. You need both elements to assist you in accomplishing your dreams. Each person's definition of success is different but each is important unto itself. Only by succeeding can we be happy and satisfied. Each person has every right to succeed with their dreams, but these dreams will never happen as long as Harold is in control. Live life the way you would a poker game. Enjoy the thrill, the passion, and the excitement."

As Gary finished his speech, there was complete silence from the computer. It was as if the whole world had totally lost power. Gary and Jack glanced at each other. The lack of sound was shocking. They feared that they had gone too far and maybe Americans weren't ready to hear what he said.

Suddenly, a grand cheer poured forth. The sound of one massive round of applause was deafening. The speech was a success, and their world was about to change. Americans now understood that they didn't have to live under Harold's rule. If they worked together, Harold could be defeated.

* * *

Mike's cell phone rang and he heard Allan say, "Prepare for developing news," but he wouldn't reveal anything further over the phone.

After Mark checked on Guenther, they heard a vehicle drive up. The men ran to the front window in time to see Allan and Chuck exiting the police car. Mike gripped the door handle. As soon as the men were on the porch, he opened the front screen door and let them inside.

"Boy, have we got news for you," said Allan rushing into the living room.

"Do tell," said Mike.

Smiling widely, Chuck and Allan stood in the center of the living room. Mark motioned to them to sit.

"We've arrested Harold's henchmen," said Chuck. He sat poised on the edge of his seat. "Remember how we assigned officers to guard those people on your list that had a five beside their name?"

"Those officers discovered men watching the fives," said Allan. He seemed more relaxed though he crossed and uncrossed his legs as he spoke.

"They were found hiding in black Cadillac Coupes just outside their victims' homes. They had detailed files of the person they were watching," said Chuck who read from his notes.

"We found all types of recording and listening devices in their cars as well as P30 Lite Semi Auto Pistols," said Allan.

"It was obvious they were up to no good," said Chuck. He laughed at his own joke.

"So who are these guys?" said Mark. He leaned back in his chair taking in this information. With these men out of the picture, he hoped this also meant his friends no longer had to worry about being discovered.

"No names. They're ghosts. They don't seem to be on any database. I've got their pictures," said Allan.

He retrieved a number of headshots from his black leather briefcase on the glass coffee table. He spread them out. Each revealed a blond, young man dressed in a black shirt and black jeans. There was nothing distinctive about men other than they were all blond and of average-to-tall height.

Mark and Mike glanced over the mug shots of the death squad. Neither recognized anyone, but it was obvious these men were connected.

"Did you follow those men?" Mike asked, flipping through the pictures.

"Yeah," said Chuck. "They tried to disappear into a tall office tower, but we captured them."

"We set up a surveillance at that building and checked every person who came and went. We must have charged forty men," said Allan, smiling broadly.

"And that's the extent of Harold's army?" asked Mark.

"Yes, we think so," said Allan. "They're not talking but they say more by their silence."

"So the American public is safe now?" said Mark putting down the last picture.

"Yes," said Chuck. "Everyone's safe."

With those words, the small group of men heaved a huge sigh of relief. Harold was going down, and it was only a matter of time before he was behind bars.

"What else you got?" said Mike who noticed Allan still smiling widely.

"We saved the best for last," said Allan. He pushed himself back into his chair as if to delay the good news.

Unable to bear the silence, Chuck burst out, "We've got the search warrant for the Hartley mansion."

"You did?" said Mark, sitting up.

When the two policemen nodded, the other men jumped up in unison and shook each other's hands. This was the end of Harold.

"Just one more thing," said Allan, sitting down again.

"What?" said Mike.

"That Angela Barrett woman is still missing. She's probably being held captive somewhere in the Hartley mansion," said Allan.

"Has anyone reported her missing?" said Mike.

"No one," said Allan.

"You can't find any family or friends?" asked Mark.

"Nothing. She's a dead end," said Chuck. "Have you extricated anything further from Guenther?"

"We decided to wait until after Gary's show to see how much back-up we would receive. Do you have any questions for him?" said Mike.

"Question him about Angela and the blond men," said Allan.

"Will do," said Mike.

"Good luck. We'll catch up tomorrow," said Allan.

"Good luck to you. Let us know as soon as you can identify Harold's henchmen," said Mike.

The four men stood up and shook each other's hands in silent agreement. They would continue on in this race to get to Harold before he got to them.

After Mike and Mark watched the police car leave the driveway, it was time to work on Guenther. Smiling, they picked up the death squad's pictures that Allan had left on the table.

When they opened the door to the guest bedroom, Guenther was sitting upright on the single bed. He appeared quite content and peaceful as though he had no worries in the world. However, as Mark entered the room, he tensed up.

"Good afternoon, Guenther," said Mark, wearing a ski mask over his face.

Mark then placed a ski mask over Guenther's head and tied his arms to the stiff bedposts. Only when he was sufficiently restricted did Mike enter the room, and he went right to work. "Who is Angela Barrett?"

"Angelo who?" said Guenther.

"You know who he means," said Mark.

"I'm sure you notice all the pretty women who enter the mansion," said Mike.

Guenther laughed a little and then said, "I don't look at the cleaning women."

"Aw, so you do know who she is?" Mark laughed.

Guenther didn't reply. He pulled at his restricted arms trying to worm out of the bindings.

"Is she being kept in the attic?" Mike asked.

"I have no idea who you mean."

Mike tried a different tact, "Why does Harold only hire blond men?"

"Harold doesn't hire them. Franz does."

Realizing he had said too much, Guenther brought his legs up to his chest and dug his face into his knees.

"Who's Franz?" asked Mike.

No answer.

"C'mon Guenther. You can tell us," said Mark.

No response.

"What is Franz to Harold?" said Mike.

Guenther lay still on the bed.

Exchanging looks of annoyance, Mark turned away from Mike then said, "We know you're holding Angela Barrett captive."

"So what?" said Guenther. "She's nothing to you."

"We have captured the blond men hired to kill the fives," said Mike.

Not expecting this, Guenther's head dropped.

"Harold will soon be in jail," said Mark.

"What are you going to do with me?" whispered Guenther.

"We're taking you to the police station," said Mike. "You'll go to prison for a long time."

Guenther's body began to shake. He kicked his legs up and down as if they were numb.

"Tell us what you know," said Mark.

Realizing Harold's take-over was finished, Guenther gave up and divulged everything. "Harold has been planning this for years. We met in Germany and he made me his second-in-command. Franz hired those blond men to 'take care' of all the unfaithful."

Mike and Mark were finally getting somewhere. While Mike continued to ask direct questions, Mark copied Guenther's responses onto the laptop.

After Guenther lay exhausted, the men left him alone. Mark immediately telephoned Jack at the cottage and relayed everything Guenther had told them. Jack was thrilled to learn that Harold's death squad had been captured and they were now in jail. Soon they'd be free to go home and resume their lives. It looked like it was all over.

THURSDAY

"Check," said Ted as he reached for a cigar.

Peter placed the flop on the poker table. It was Mark's turn to bet.

Mark smiled widely. He was glad to be home. It seemed like years since the guys had come together to play poker in his house. Mark checked.

Jack raised, doubling the blind.

Gary smiled at Jack. He knew he was bluffing. Gary had hit a pair of tens, but there was an ace on the table. Deciding to stay in the hunt, Gary called Jack's bet.

Ted, Peter, and Mark folded their hands.

Peter placed the turn card on the table, revealing a jack of clubs.

Jack made a large bet, which Gary quickly called. He threw the same amount of chips into the center of the poker table.

Peter tossed the river onto the table and revealed a two of diamonds.

Jack made another large bet, which Gary happily called showing two pair (jacks and tens). Jack had ace three, only one pair. Smiling, Gary gathered all the chips and placed them in his pile.

"So, it's all over," said Peter, finishing his beer.

"Yes it is," Ted said. He left his chair to retrieve another round of beer.

"The police searched Harold's mansion and found Angela being held captive. Along with everything we have provided them, Harold has been indicted for treason, kidnapping, and extortion," said Mark, stubbing out his cigar.

"He's finished," said Gary still piling his chips.

"What did you do with Guenther?" asked Jack while he accepted a cold beer from Ted. He opened it and drank deeply.

"Dropped him off at the police station where he's being held on charges," said Mark. He gathered the cards and shuffled them.

When Allan and Chuck informed Mike that the police department was prepared to descend upon Harold's mansion and complete a full scale search, the men agreed that holding Guenther was no longer necessary. He had sunk into a deep depression after he was told that Harold was in jail. With no life outside of Harold's controlled environment, Guenther became pitiful, proving to Mike and Mark that nothing further could be gained by keeping him hostage. Mike took him to the local police station.

"He must have given in pretty fast?" said Gary, opening the beer bottle.

"Yes. As soon as he realized how much we knew, he divulged everything," said Mark.

After taking a huge gulp of beer, Gary took the cards from Mark and shuffled them a bit. He then handed out two cards to each man.

Peter called the blind and everyone limped in.

After the flop, the first to bet was Jack who threw in a few chips. Ted called but the rest of the guys folded their hands.

Unable to contain himself any longer, Gary said, "I've got some great news."

"Well, spill the beans," said Jack.

"Anne's pregnant."

"Is she?" The guys replied in unison.

With a huge, glowing smile on his face, Gary nodded. "She told me the news this morning. A doctor's appointment is scheduled for next week but she's sure."

"This calls for cognac," said Mark.

He reached out to the wooden cabinet against the wall and retrieved a bottle. Mark handed out glasses to each of his friends.

"To Anne," said the men, raising then clicking their glasses together.

"And now to me," said Mark who remained holding his glass up high.

"Do tell," said Gary.

"Maggie's moving in."

The poker buddies burst out laughing. The guys had liked Maggie. She had fit in well with their little group, but they were surprised at the advancement of their relationship. They had all considered Mark a confirmed bachelor but were glad to be proven wrong.

"When's the auspicious date?" said Peter.

"This weekend. We agreed that she should quit her job at Starbucks."

This was a complete change. Mark had always been wonderful with their wives, but the poker buddies never believed that he would ever have one of his own. He seemed happy and content with his bachelor life. Obviously, their adventure had brought out a big transformation.

"Have you ever heard back from that government official?" asked Ted.

"Yes. Landry sent me an email explaining that the government will be weeding out any negative element and will reorganize themselves. They've had quite a shock," said Gary.

"Yes. I'm sure," said Ted.

"So? What happens now?" said Peter.

"Hopefully a society which is more in tune with reality," said Jack.

"And a happier one," said Gary.

"A much happier one," Mark said smiling.

The men laughed remembering their courage and bravery in defeating the dreaded Harold Hartley. They had provided Americans with a new lease on life where they could only better themselves and live without fear.

It was a new world, one based on honesty and equality.

After living around the world, Patty returned to Ontario where she grew up. She has been writing all her life, starting with poems as a child. A few years ago, she began writing novels. Her first book is non-fiction, *Shall We Chat?* Also published are *Locker Rooms*, a fiction/fantasy/paranormal, *That Truthful Place*, fiction/science fiction/YA, *A Discerning Heart*, fiction/historical/romantic/fantasy/adventure. Soon to be published, *Devouring Time*, fiction/ mystery.

www.pattylesser.com

Acknowlegements

A huge thanks to Andi Combo-Floyd (www.andlit.com). Without her, I would never have been able to complete this novel.

Big thanks to Nate Hendley for his great editing services and to Miriam and Youngman Brown for proofreading the novel.

An additional thanks to Miriam for all her support and for driving me to all my signings. Thanks to Rivka for all her work on my website.

52672459R10161

Made in the USA
Charleston, SC
23 February 2016